"I WANT YOU TO STAY WITH ME TONIGHT . . ."

Jan had sensed that somehow they would end up this way. "Kiss me," she invited, her lips parting as she pulled his head down, her tongue boldly investigating the hard corners of his mouth.

"You are wonderful," Dave whispered, brushing intoxicating kisses across her eyes, her cheeks, her throat, before reclaiming her moist, open lips in a kiss that exposed his rising, burning need. His fingers unzipped her dress, caressing the bare skin of her back. Overwhelmed, she gave herself up to the blissful heat his hands were creating on her body. . . .

D1737292

JOANN ROBB is an incurable optimist, believing steadfastly in happy endings. She lives in Arizona with her husband and her teenage son, both of whom she fell in love with at first sight. She loves anything to do with flying, the desert, sunshine, and yellow flowers. She is the author of two other Rapture Romances, *Dreamlover* and *Stardust and Diamonds*.

Dear Reader:

We at Rapture Romance hope you will continue to enjoy our four books each month as much as we enjoy bringing them to you. Our commitment remains strong to giving you only the best, by well-known favorite authors and exciting new writers.

We've used the comments and opinions we've heard from *you*, the reader, to make our selections, so please keep writing to us. Your letters have already helped us bring you better books—the kind you want—and we appreciate and depend on them. Of course, we are always happy to forward mail to our authors—writers need to hear from their fans!

And don't miss any of the inside story on Rapture. To tell you about upcoming books, introduce you to the authors, and give you a behind-the-scenes look at romance publishing, we've started a *free* newsletter, *The Rapture Reader*. Just write to the address below, and we will be happy to send you each issue.

Happy reading!

The Editors
Rapture Romance
New American Library
1633 Broadway
New York, NY 10019

STERLING DECEPTIONS

by

JoAnn Robb

RAPTURE ROMANCE

NEW AMERICAN LIBRARY

NAL BOOKS ARE AVAILABLE AT QUANTITY DISCOUNTS
WHEN USED TO PROMOTE PRODUCTS OR SERVICES.
FOR INFORMATION PLEASE WRITE TO PREMIUM MARKETING DIVISION,
NEW AMERICAN LIBRARY, 1633 BROADWAY,
NEW YORK, NEW YORK 10019.

SIGNET, SIGNET CLASSIC, MENTOR, PLUME, MERIDIAN AND NAL BOOKS
are published by New American Library,
1633 Broadway, New York, New York 10019

First Printing, April, 1984

1 2 3 4 5 6 7 8 9

PRINTED IN THE UNITED STATES OF AMERICA

*To my sisters—Laurie, Sue, and BJ,
whose pride in me could never equal
my pride in them.*

Chapter One

☙

Jan Baxter cringed as Rod Stewart began singing a spirited song about two young lovers. She jerked the tape out of her car's tape deck and inserted a jazz ensemble instead, losing herself in the sweet, teasing notes of the saxophone. She told herself it was fatigue, and not the too many margaritas at last night's birthday party, that had her out of sorts. Fatigue and the odd sensation that life was passing her by.

She'd never been a young lover, such as the song portrayed. She'd been too busy winning medals. Medals that were proving to be little consolation on these long, lonely nights. At one time, her only goal in life had been to obtain an Olympic diving medal. Well, she'd done that long ago and was now busily involved in training the next generation of Olympic hopefuls at one of the most prestigious diving clubs in the country. Jan knew it was a life many would envy. Yet something was definitely wrong. She'd become uneasy lately, jumpy, suddenly dissatisfied with what she'd always considered an ideal life.

Jan was on her way to Phoenix to check out a youngster who'd applied to her San Diego diving and swimming club. Jimmy Cassidy's credentials were impressive, and this weekend he was participating in the Arizona finals. Jan had chosen to drive, taking the opportunity to break in her new car. As an added bonus, the trip across the miles of open land seemed to be effectively clearing out the cobwebs from last night's festivities.

She was nearing the outskirts of the sprawling resort city when she saw a car pulled off the highway, the hood up and a white cloth tied to the antenna in the universal distress signal. A man leaned against the side of the small car, looking hopefully at the passing traffic.

Jan slowed down, eyeing the stranded motorist. He doesn't look like a dangerous man, she thought. He was tall, or at least appeared so next to the low roof of the car. And lean. Her green eyes, used to appraising athletes' bodies for fitness, noted that the lanky frame had not an ounce of spare flesh on it. His legs, she noted in her quick perusal as her car passed him by, seemed to stretch forever.

Jan Baxter was a cautious person by nature, never stopping for hitchhikers. But the desert heat and the downcast expression that appeared in her rearview mirror conspired against common sense and had her pulling over to the side of the highway and backing up.

She leaned across the wide seat to roll down the window on the passenger side as he came running toward her. He had a loose-boned, easy gait. No, not at all dangerous, she reconfirmed as the grinning face appeared framed in the open window.

"Can I help you?" she asked.

Ginger-colored hair ruffled in the breeze as his blue eyes echoed his embarrassed smile. "You wouldn't happen to know anything about car engines, would you?"

Jan shook her head. "Not a thing. Except that it's advisable to have the man check the water and oil once in a while. From there—it's anyone's guess."

"Would you know how far it is to a garage?"

She shook her head. "No. But if you get in, we can probably find one together." She pulled up the button, unlocking the door so he could join her.

"Boy, this is great of you," he said as he leaned back against the rich burgundy velour seat, stretching a pair of incredibly long legs out in front of him. "It was getting hot out there. I kept remembering all those bleached steer skulls I used to see in the old Saturday matinees, wondering if that's how I was going to end up."

"I would think," she replied, to her own shock and discomfort, "that anyone who's accumulated enough wealth to own a sporty little BMW like yours should have the intelligence to learn something about the way it works. Aren't European cars supposed to be very temperamental?"

Terrific, Jan, she thought, cringing. Just because you've run into more than your share of creeps with foreign cars is no reason to jump all over the poor guy. In her thirty years of living in San Diego, Jan had met too many representatives of that breed of professional California bachelor—tanned chests covered with rows of gold chains. She'd often wondered if they ever realized just how foolish those chains looked with swim trunks. They all drove low-slung European sports cars with the rearview mirrors tilted so they could continually check their permed, blond-streaked hair. Jan had the grace to grimace at her outburst, however. Nothing like wearing your prejudices right out on your sleeve, she scolded herself.

He looked at her across the wide seat, obviously surprised by her short tone. "In the first place," he said slowly, "I haven't accumulated a lot of wealth. I'm just a poor working stiff. So if you're thinking about rolling me and leaving me out in the desert, forget it. You'd only get about a hundred bucks in traveler's checks, an American Express card that already has more charges on it than you'd care to end up paying, and the keys to a car that won't, at the moment, budge an inch.

"As for that car," he continued calmly, "I bought it for a good price from a UPI reporter in Munich who had twenty-four hours to divest himself of excess baggage before taking off for the jungles of El Salvador. Besides," he challenged, "do you have any idea what a little beauty like this would cost in Europe? Not to mention the cost of feeding it the greedy quantities of overpriced gasoline it would consume?"

His roving blue gaze took in the lush interior of her full-size American convertible. Jan knew that it was an extravagance and that many people would have spent the money on a trendy little sports car instead, but she'd been pleased to see the return of the rag top and she liked the roomy comfort it gave her five-foot-ten-inch frame.

"Touché," she murmured. "I'm sorry. I was out of line. Bad night last night," she offered as a partial excuse, knowing as she did so that her behavior had still been unwarranted. "Of course it's entirely your business what type of car you drive."

The light turned red and Jan looked to the right, only to be greeted by an absolutory grin and the brightest, most crystal-blue eyes she'd ever seen.

"Or don't drive," he reminded her. "It's a honey of a car, but once the BMW decided to stop, there wasn't a thing I could do to persuade it. Including a rather colorful round of cursing, which undoubtedly frightened off more than one prospective Good Samaritan."

"Perhaps you should've tried cursing in German."

Approval lit the blue eyes. "What a great idea! Why didn't I think of that?"

Jan was caught for a span of several seconds in

the gleaming blue pools as her car idled smoothly. Then the light changed to green and her attention was forced back to the roadway. She started through the intersection.

"There's a garage." He pointed to the right. "Sign says he works on imports."

Jan signaled, turning into the driveway of the garage. "Should I wait and see what they say?" For some unknown reason, she didn't want him to disappear from her life. Not quite yet.

He'd opened the car door, his long legs already swiveling in the direction of the pavement. His keen blue eyes lingered on her, moving from her crisp, chin-length dark hair with its bright streaks of sun to the green eyes with their slightly upward slant, down the slim, straight nose to her lips. They lingered there for a moment, as if imagining the taste and feel of them, before continuing down to her slim body, clad in white jeans and a sea-green T-shirt. As an assertion of femininity, shiny pink toenails peeked from the sandal resting on the brake pedal, gleaming like jewels against the dark tan of her skin. His gaze rose back to her eyes as if trying to read a message there. The roomy interior of the car suddenly filled with a curiously expectant air and Jan realized she was actually holding her breath.

"What's the matter, Mac? We're closin' up here."

A burly bear of a man came lumbering toward them, wiping his hands on a grease-coated rag. The intense gaze was broken and the stranger turned, unfolding his long, lanky frame from the car.

"I've got a car stopped down the road," he answered. "Think you could tow it in for me?"

"Only if we do it right now. My mother-in-law is coming to supper tonight, and if I'm too late, the old bat'll never believe I had an excuse. And believe me, guy, I'm too old and too fat to spend any more nights on the couch."

Jan's stranger, which is how she was beginning to think of him, turned back to her, bending down to look into the open doorway. "I really do appreciate it, Ms.—?"

"Ba-Banning," she stammered, instantly wondering what inner demon had just caused her to lie about her name.

The crystal eyes warmed to a deep sapphire. "Thanks for everything."

"It was nothing."

"Nothing," she repeated as she pulled back out into the street, watching him climb into the tow truck with the bulky driver. "Nothing but a brief, impersonal encounter. You'll never see that man again."

Jan Baxter told herself all that. But she couldn't tell herself why she'd lied about her name; she didn't know.

The sun was a high, blazing ball of fire in the sky, its rays reflecting off the brilliant turquoise of the Olympic-size swimming pool. As each diver plunged into the cool depths, a spray of water rose into the air, every droplet turning to a sparkling gemstone in the rainbow created by the diffused light.

Jan had left her motel room early this morning, arriving for the first round of the competition by seven o'clock. It was now twelve-thirty in the afternoon and she was considering how nice it would feel to dive into the inviting blue water herself.

A wonderfully familiar, rich voice broke into her thoughts. "I thought that was you down here."

She turned, allowing the silly, welcoming smile to stay on her lips. "How's your car?"

"Still in intensive care. Marvin, the hulk with the

mother-in-law, swears he's taking care of it. Mumbled something about only the best as he picked up the phone to order parts. Does that mean what I think it does?"

Jan nodded, still smiling. Stop that, she instructed her facial muscles. But they seemed to have developed a mind of their own. "It's going to be expensive," she agreed.

He groaned. "That's what I was afraid of." Blue eyes scanned the stands around them, squinting slightly in the glaring sunshine. "Are you alone?"

"Not now." Jan scooted over, patting the wooden bench beside her.

"Is this what brought you to Phoenix?" He nodded in the direction of the divers.

Still uncertain of her reasons, Jan preferred not to divulge too much about herself. She assured herself it was only to prevent the inevitable questions about her Olympic experiences.

"No. I'm just passing time," she lied once more. "And you?"

"My motel's down the street. I was taking a walk and saw the crowd. Thought I'd see what was going on."

"Oh."

They returned their attention to the diving, but Jan's mind was aware only of the man beside her. She knew every time he breathed, every time his long bronze lashes fluttered over his intense blue eyes. And when he shifted his long legs, brushing her thigh with his, she felt as if she'd just been jolted with a charge of electricity.

"I've got an idea."

She turned, knowing she was going to accept the bright invitation gleaming in his eyes. "What's your idea?"

"Since you're just passing time—and I just want

to be with someone—why don't we pass the time together? Somewhere else?"

She turned back to see the scores being held up by the judges. Scores didn't matter. She'd seen enough. Jimmy Cassidy was terrific, and if he wanted to give up any semblance of a normal life and his parents were willing and able to make the sacrifices necessary, she'd recommend his acceptance at La Conquista. She slipped her hand into the one he'd extended.

"I think that's a brilliant idea."

"Now it's your turn."

Jan turned to him as they reached her car, realizing as they stood together that he was very tall. She actually had to look up at him. "My turn?"

"You thought up the German cussing." He ticked off, using his long fingers. "I thought up getting out of here. Now it's your turn for the next bright idea. I like to share everything right down the middle."

"All the decisions?"

"Of course. It's only fair. That way, if something goes wrong, I can only take half the blame."

"I've got just the place," she decided. She headed the car into traffic, driving through Phoenix and finally pulling into an area of lush green grass, tall mature trees, and a cool, long, winding lagoon.

"When was the last time you paddled a canoe?" she asked.

"You read my mind."

Jan took the keys from the ignition after parking, eyeing him skeptically. "Sure."

"No, really. I was just thinking that you were the type of woman a man would want to serenade on a sultry summer afternoon. It's too bad I can't sing. I'm afraid I'd just scare you off."

His blue eyes were lit with a deep glow that paid compliments, and Jan felt confused as she searched the friendly features for a joke. Was he teasing?

She'd never been the type of woman any man considered serenading. That was always saved for the soft, ultrafeminine types.

"That's a good line," she remarked casually, swinging her long legs out of the car. "May I use it some time?"

"Of course," came the easy answer. "You can even use it on me. In fact, if you can carry a tune, pretty lady, I'll be happy to let you serenade me. You'll discover one of the most lovable things about me is that I'm very agreeable."

"If you're claiming part credit," she warned, "the idea still counts as mine."

"Of course," he repeated, taking her hand in his as they walked up to the canoe rental.

The paddle cut through the water with a clean swish as they made their way around the cool, man-made lagoon. "This was your second terrific idea," he acknowledged. "Are you from Phoenix?"

"No. Tucson." There she went again, she rued, wishing she could bite back the answer. Why in heaven's name did she keep lying like this? What did it matter?

"How did you know this was here?"

"I've visited Phoenix a few times. Encanto Park is one of my favorite places."

"Encanto. Enchanting," he translated. "It fits. I can see why you like it. It's peaceful here, a green oasis in the middle of a bustling desert city. I like it, too."

"I'm glad." Jan smiled at him, enjoying the moment.

There was a comfortable silence as they slid through the dark water, watching the flock of ducks bobbing for food, wide orange feet wagging in the air as broad yellow beaks worked through the grasses under the surface.

"My turn," he said as he took her hand, helping her out of the tippy canoe.

"Your turn?"

"For the idea," he reminded her patiently. "Follow me. I spied this while I was paddling."

He led her through the wooded green of the park to the children's amusement section, shushing her protest as he bought two tickets. Then he pulled her to a gaily colored carousel that was filling the afternoon air with a wonderful, strident calliope sound.

"It's marvelous!" Jan stood and gazed in thrilled wonder as they waited. The confection of mirrors and gaudy carvings whirled on, the bright wooden steeds flew by with flaring nostrils and fiery eyes, and the carved wooden manes seemed to toss in the wind.

The raucous calliope music slowed in cadence with the spinning carousel as it came to a stop, allowing them to board.

"My lady, your chariot awaits," he murmured, his hands on either side of her waist as he lifted her up, sidesaddle, onto a prancing white, rose-garlanded charger. Before she could protest, he had swung up behind her, holding his hand over hers on the tall polished brass pole.

They began to move, the stallion riding up and down in time to the music, increasing speed. Jan's back was against his chest and his arm curled around her waist as they rode the carousel, Jan laughing with gleeful elation. She didn't want to tell him she'd never in her life done something as simple as ride a merry-go-round. How could he ever relate to the child she'd been? It was too complicated a story for the pleasure she was receiving from this sun-drenched afternoon. She allowed her head to rest back on his shoulder as she laughed, loving the ridiculous-looking horse, the horrible music, and the feel of his body close to hers.

He took both her hands in his, turning her toward him as they left the carousel, looking down into her flushed, merry face. His expression revealed that he felt immensely pleased with himself.

"I think I'm batting a thousand. You liked that," he said.

The radiance on Jan's shining countenance could have easily been mistaken for a woman who'd just been given the deed to a South African diamond mine, and not a simple ride on a carousel.

"I loved it," she bubbled, eyeing the small train whose whistle warned them off the track. "And it's my turn. Come for a ride with me?" Her emerald eyes danced as they coaxed him toward the red-roofed station.

"Anywhere." He grinned as they ran to make the train before it departed for its short tour of the park.

"You must be feeling better."

Jan's mind had been drifting, drinking in the sheer pleasure of this day, and she had to pull her attention back to his casually issued statement. They were strolling along the banks of the lagoon, her hand fitting into his perfectly.

"Better than what?"

"You said yesterday you were recovering from a bad night. You seem in a better mood today."

"I really am sorry about that," Jan apologized again for her unwarranted attack. "Everything just seemed to catch up with me. I swear I'll never have another birthday as long as I live."

"So that's all it was. You shouldn't have made the mistake of analyzing your life when you looked back."

She came to an abrupt halt, looking up at him. "How did you know that's what I'd been doing?"

He shrugged. "It's only human nature. We all do it and I think it's probably a big mistake. I've got a terrific idea! Oh—wait a minute, pretty lady— shelve that idea for a more immediate one."

He changed his mind suddenly, leading her toward the red-and-white-striped awning of the sandwich stand. "We'll discuss it over lunch, O.K.?"

Jan wondered why he'd even bothered to ask. She seemed unable to deny this man anything today. She nodded, stunned as he ordered two pastrami and Swiss on rye, two orders of coleslaw, and double portions of macaroni salad.

"Wait a minute," he decided suddenly, "could you put some corned beef on those, too?"

"Sure." The young man behind the counter began unwrapping the sandwiches.

Jan found her voice as the clerk began slicing the pink meat.

"Do you have an army stashed in the bushes? I couldn't possibly eat all this."

"And that cheesecake," he continued, ignoring her protest. "Is it fresh?"

"Yes sir."

"Great. Two slices. The kind with the cherries on top."

"What in the world are you doing? You've ordered enough to feed everyone in this park."

"You're not allowing me my idea," he protested, paying for the lunch. He handed her two glasses of iced tea to carry as he picked up the heavily laden cardboard box. "It's my turn and this is my next great idea."

"Some great idea," Jan muttered under her breath. "It's a good thing we went canoeing *before* lunch. I think we'd swamp the thing if we actually eat all this food you've bought."

He held out a slice of crisp green pickle, encouraging her to take a bite. "Don't be a spoilsport. You could eat ten times this amount and still have an absolutely gorgeous figure."

Jan could feel the flush rising in her cheeks as his blue eyes moved appreciatively over her body. She thought about describing her work clothes, how the scant tank suits she wore didn't hide an ounce. But that would involve revealing what she did for a living, which in turn would bring up her true identity, and then she'd be forced to explain those outrageous lies. No, she decided, the best thing to do was eat the damn food and work it off with extra laps once she returned to San Diego.

"I know it's your turn," he said on a happy, fulfilled sigh, gathering up the empty wrappings, "but I had an idea going before we stopped for a bite."

A bite? Where did the man put it all? The food had been vacuumed up as if it were absolutely normal behavior, as if he consumed the caloric intake of the entire third world every day. The man must have fantastic metabolism, she thought with some envy as her gaze moved over his lithe frame.

She'd given up on finishing the herculean lunch long ago and had been content to toss crumbs to the ducks, which were swimming in lazy circles near the bank.

"If it involves food," she groaned, "don't tell me."

"It's simple enough. We'll form a partnership. You agree to take my mind off all the dreary things on *my* birthdays and I'll do the same for you."

What in the world was he talking about? He knew her birthday had been two days ago. Once this day ended, she'd never see the man again. She didn't even know his name, she realized with a jolt. Or where he'd come from before appearing alongside the deserted desert highway. Or where he was headed. And she certainly didn't know where he'd be a year from now.

She was saved from answering as a pair of geese swam up, their strong beaks snapping as they chased away her pastrami-eating ducks. They waddled up onto the bank, grabbing greedily at the leftover sandwich. Jan gave a small shriek as they began to hiss, unwilling to give up once they'd devoured the last of the dark bread. She scrambled up onto the table, throwing little bits of macaroni from the plastic container.

"Don't just stand there laughing," she complained, her own laughter breaking through the stern expression she tried to hold. "Do something!"

Her breath caught in her lungs as he reached up and lifted her off the table, holding her firmly against him as he slowly lowered her to the ground. Her hands were resting on his shoulders and for a long, silent moment he held her gaze, recreating that golden moment they'd experienced yesterday. Then the geese honked, moving toward them with ungainly but quick movements. He pitched the rest of the leftovers into the wire trash container and pulled her off down the path.

"Are we running away from a pair of overweight geese?"

"Of course not." His bright blue eyes scolded her in the friendliest of fashions. "We're simply attacking in the opposite direction."

The rest of the afternoon passed in a wonderful rosy haze. They contributed to the amusement of an entire preschool class as he made their seat swing while they were perched atop the ferris wheel, making Jan screech and hang on to him for dear life.

"Remind me to buy a fistful of tickets for that thing," he said as they exited. "Boy, I wish I'd known it was that easy to entice a pretty woman onto your lap when I was seventeen."

Her eyes were brilliant emeralds. "Oh, I bet you didn't need any help when you were seventeen. I can see you now, fighting the girls off with a stick."

A strange expression darkened his face for a moment, so fleeting that Jan thought she'd imagined it. "Not exactly." Then that magical grin brightened his features once again, rivaling the Arizona sun for warmth.

"Let's try a couple of those bows and arrows," he suggested, his hand resting in light possession on her back as he led her toward the clubhouse. "With any luck we could end up having a roasted goose for dinner."

Chapter Two

❦

"How do you want to handle dinner?"

"Dinner?"

"Do we go to your place, so you can change first, or mine? You're the one with the car." A slight, apologetic quirk appeared on his lips.

"My place first," Jan decided. Then, not wanting to appear too eager, she added a qualifying statement. "Or I can drop you off at your motel and pick you up later."

"You just blew a pretty good run, pretty lady," he warned her lightly, running his palm down her jean-clad thigh as she maneuvered the car through traffic. Jan almost jammed on the brake at the warmth he'd incited. "I don't want to give up the pleasure of your company for a single moment we have left today. We'll get you all tidied up, then see what we can do with me. Of course, in your case, we're starting with a lot better raw material."

Jan turned her head, favoring him with a smile. Not traditionally handsome, he had a bold, ready grin and those incredible eyes. His ginger-colored hair was cut moderately short, as if to control the crisp, natural wave. The same hair graced his arms and legs, but there it had lightened to a burnished red-gold. She wondered if it was on his chest and what it would feel like to run her fingers through its softness. Jan moved her judicious gaze down the tall frame, following the lithe build. She'd had to look up into those dancing blue eyes today. He must be—what—six-two, -three? Hmm, no, his raw material was just fine.

It said something about his easygoing personality that she didn't feel any strain entering her motel room with him. He'd given her every indication that he found her appealing, but Jan knew there'd be no wrestling matches when he saw the king-size bed that dominated the small room.

"I'll just take a quick shower and be right out."

"No hurry. I'll watch the news." He sank down onto the end of the bed, fiddling with the dial of the color television.

Jan reached the closet, pulling out the dress she'd packed only because it had been a birthday present from her best friend, who'd insisted she take it along. "It'll bring you luck," Maggie Gallagher had insisted, shoving it into Jan's hands. It wasn't something that Jan would ever buy for herself, which was exactly why Maggie had purchased it, she realized with a grin. The dress was made of crisp white cotton eyelet in a halter design. With a full, gathered skirt, it was incredibly cool-looking and unabashedly romantic. It also showed her deep tan off to a bronzed glory, she realized, checking her reflection in the bathroom mirror before rejoining him.

He was engrossed in the sports cast and Jan joined him on the end of the bed, noting with satisfaction that Jimmy Cassidy had captured the gold medal at today's meet. He had quite a future ahead of him, she thought, if he was willing to go all out for it. And she knew only too well the meaning and results of that.

She'd given up adolescence. Given up dating. God knows, she'd given up the sexual revolution. It had passed Jan by while she'd been perfecting a

triple-twist back dive. It had recently occurred to
Jan that she was doing exactly the same thing she'd
been doing at seven years old. She got up. Went to
the pool. Worked. Returned home. Went to bed.
And the next day she'd go through the same routine
all over again. Day in and day out. She'd seen
trained seals with more variety in their lives.

"You win." The blue eyes glittered to life as they
feasted on her.

"Win what?"

"Me, I think. Unless you'd consider that a booby
prize."

An elusive smile crossed her lips as she allowed
his gaze to capture and hold hers.

"Never the booby prize," she murmured. "But
why am I the lucky winner?" A flush appeared on
her cheeks. She didn't know how to ask this next
question, but surely it was time. "And now that
you've mentioned it, I don't know *who* I've won."

Something unreadable flickered for an instant in
his eyes. "Dave Barrie," he said as his long body
uncoiled from the mattress, extending a downward
hand to her.

She took it, rising to stand a whisper away from
the solid wall of his chest.

"And you won," he answered genially, "because
that dress is by far the winning idea of the day!"

"The night's still young," Jan protested, amazing herself with her husky, provocative tone. "Perhaps you shouldn't concede. Quite yet."

Blue eyes didn't move from green as he searched
for the message hidden in her emerald depths.

"Perhaps I won't," Dave allowed on a low, deep
note. "Not just yet."

He was staying at a motel a few miles away, close
to the pool where she'd met him that afternoon. Jan
handed him the keys, inviting him to drive as they
left her room. She didn't sit as close to him as she

would have preferred, but neither did she hug the door. Instead, she settled for somewhere in the middle of the velour bench seat, turning slightly so she could watch him as he drove. She put a Paul McCartney tape into the tape deck, humming softly along with it as her eyes drank in his profile.

His nose was slightly pug and looked as if it might have been broken at some time in his life. The lines fanning his eyes appeared as though they'd been etched there by more smiles than the average human shares in a lifetime. His gaze was directed out the front windshield, but Jan knew that those long, curly bronze lashes framed eyes that were so brilliantly blue they could have been plucked from a clear summer sky.

"You're making concentration difficult, you know." Dave slanted a keen blue gaze in her direction.

"I know."

"And you don't care that you're beginning to make me incredibly nervous with that beautiful emerald gaze?"

"I care." Jan's smooth, grave tones swirled around them. "I just can't seem to stop," she answered truthfully.

She watched him expel a deep breath, returning his attention to the traffic circling Moon Mountain.

"I know the feeling," he replied into the soft, crooning ballad playing in the confines of the car. "Very well."

"That was fast."

Jan smiled a greeting as Dave emerged from the bathroom, clad in a white silk shirt and brown dress slacks. He was barefoot and pulled a pair of socks from a drawer before crossing over to where she stood.

"I had plenty of incentive. I told you I didn't want to leave you. I was getting lonely in there."

"I'm sorry."

He gave her another one of those vivid grins. "If I'd known that, I would've called you in to scrub my back."

"Aren't your own arms long enough?"

Dave tossed the socks onto a chair and slid his arms about her waist as he pulled her to him and his ginger head lowered.

"Long enough," he murmured just before his lips reached hers, "for everything that counts. Like holding you, pretty lady."

His breath played warmly against her mouth as his lips found hers in a deliberately slow, tantalizing kiss. His tongue traced the full outline of her lips, then ran across her teeth, before gently probing her mouth with its sensuous tip. His hands spanned her waist, drawing her into him as his mouth moved against hers, revealing a hunger he'd been carrying since she'd first rolled down the car window to ask if she could help.

Jan's mouth acquiesced to his sweet demands, answering with a long, quivering breath that revealed her matching desire. Her fingers thrust through his crisp, tawny hair, feeling the moisture left from the shower. She cradled his head in her palms as she pulled him nearer, offering him the sweet nectar of her lips.

His hands roamed the silky bare skin of her back and he seemed pleased with the answering moans escaping the lips that moved so sweetly under his. For long-drawn-out moments, they were content to explore the blissful heights a mere kiss can reach when two people come together at that perfect moment in time.

"Dinner," he murmured against her dark, silky hair.

"Mmm." Jan moved against him, in no hurry to go anywhere.

"I promised to feed you."

Dave's voice was growing more ragged by the minute and Jan could feel the sharp intake of breath as she slid her fingers through the buttons of the silk shirt. The muscles of his chest moved under her fingertips and his tongue moved in response to the fires she was stoking within him, teasing the sensitive hollow of her ear.

"I'm not hungry," she whispered, pressing her lips to the base of his throat, exposed by the open collar. "Not for food, Dave."

The intimate kiss brought a deep groan from his chest, one she could feel rumbling under her exploring fingertips.

"I want you to stay with me tonight, Jan." He brushed intoxicating kisses across her eyes, her cheeks, her throat, before reclaiming her parted, moist lips in a kiss that exposed his rising, burning need.

His hand moved from her back, under the white eyelet to capture the fullness of her breasts, which were unfettered under the cool white cotton.

"You just won," she gasped, closing her eyes to the sheer pleasure. Her head was thrown back, her full pink lips parted in ecstasy from his touch.

Dave's deep vibrating voice groaned an inarticulate litany of thanksgiving against those inviting lips. To her, to his amazing luck, to whatever fates and gods had brought her to him. His long fingers moved to the back of her neck to untie the halter top. When the front of the dress fell to her waist, he bent, taking her breasts in his palms as his lips explored her beauty. His tongue circled the pouting nipples, each in turn, with feathery little strokes, the lines at his eyes deepening as he lifted his head to look up at her.

"They like me," he said softly, indicating the tanned buds, which were hard and seeming to reach for his continued touch.

"They'd be fools not to," she whispered.

"That makes us even." His lips burned her skin, creating a fire that spread through her middle—flashing, sparking heat that curled outward in little tongues. "Because I think they're wonderful." His lips continued their evocative caress until she thought she'd faint with pleasure. Finally releasing her ravished breasts, Dave rose to his full height.

"And you're wonderful," he breathed deeply, his eyes darkening with a smoky intensity. "If I ever see the UPI guy who sold me that car, I'm going to kiss him."

"Kiss me instead," Jan invited, her lips parting as she pulled his head down, her tongue boldly investigating the hard corners of his mouth.

His fingers were busy on her back, unzipping the dress, allowing it to drop into a crisp white cloud on the carpeting. Jan stepped out of it, hating to break the close contact their bodies had established. In concession to the desert heat, she was wearing only a pair of white bikini panties and she heard his gasp of pleasure as he held her at arms' length.

"My God," Dave whispered hoarsely, "you're a goddess. A tall, bronzed goddess."

His hands traced her high cheekbones, moving down her throat where his thumbs caressed her pulse spot. His lips covered the throbbing blood beat, as if to synchronize the rate of his own heart with hers.

His long fingers trailed fire across her collarbone before moving down to circle her taut, uplifted breasts. Though her figure could never be described as voluptuous, years of athletic training had made her breasts firm and the privacy of back-yard tanning had left them a deep honey-gold. Dave kissed them almost reverently, as if paying homage before allowing his fingertips their continued exploration.

He ran them over her rib cage, feeling the tensing of firm muscles under his touch. Jan was aflame with a searing desire as his hands moved, his palms following the slim line of her waist before curving outward with a slight flaring for her hips. He knelt, his hands spanning the taut muscles of her tanned thighs as he left a fiery path down one firm leg, repeating the same trail upward on the other. Jan was growing weaker by the moment, and she put her hands on his shoulders to steady herself.

"You're perfect," he breathed heavily, rising to take her hand and lead her to the bed. He lay beside her, swift deft movements divesting her of the last wispy barrier to his touch. "A magnificent specimen of womankind, Jan Banning."

The name jolted her for an instant and suddenly Jan realized why her unruly mind had kept issuing those false statements. She'd known, from that long golden moment at the stoplight, that somehow they'd end up this way. It had seemed as inevitable as the rising sun each morning, and the only way she could ever allow herself to go through with this unbelievably atypical behavior was to keep the affair anonymous. It was the only way she'd permit herself to satisfy this incredible yearning for him, knowing that they'd never meet again, that she'd never have to face him and account for this uninhibited behavior. For while Jan Baxter would never respond in such a manner to a total stranger, Jan Banning was bound by no rules. The woman didn't even exist. How could she be held responsible?

The puzzling riddle solved, Jan forbade her mind to consider it further. Instead she gave herself up to the blissful heat his hands were creating as they searched her body, seeking out erogenous zones she'd never dreamed existed.

Jan's hands reached out to unfasten the buttons of his shirt, freeing him from the light silk and allowing her fingers to delight in the gingery hair she'd known would greet her. Dave made a muffled groan in his throat as her hands moved down to the waistband of the slim dress slacks and she slid the smooth zipper down with a purposeful, unhurried motion.

He arched toward her as her hand skimmed across the taut, hard abdomen and beyond, and Jan was amazed at the way she could deepen his hunger for her. He took long, deep drafts of air as her hand moved inside the waistband of his briefs, her fluttering fingers causing immediate response.

Dave left her reluctantly to stand beside the bed, his burning gaze not leaving hers as he stripped off the slacks and the low-rise navy briefs that did nothing to hide his arousal. Jan lay on her back, looking up at him in wonder.

Dressed, Dave Barrie was tall and lean, appearing almost lanky in build. But without the camouflage of clothing, he was rock-hard, his body a succession of long, whipcord muscles that were, at this moment, glistening in the dim light of the room with a fine film of perspiration. Now there was raw material! As perfect a masculinity as any man could hope to possess. Her body moved instinctively, her hips lifting in sensuous invitation, her arms outstretched, offering him all that she was.

The mattress sank under his weight as Dave rejoined her, lying on his side, his head propped up on one hand so he could allow his fingers and eyes to trace her womanly curves.

"Thank you, Jan." His tone was strained, but serious. "Thank you for everything."

His lips then moved to follow the teasing path his fingers had forged, his tongue making delicate forays into all the sensitive hollows of her body, causing Jan to gasp and twist against him.

"Oh, Dave, thank *you*," she expelled on a ragged sigh, wishing that every inch of her could feel his touch at the same time. No man had ever made her feel as much a woman as Dave Barrie was doing at this moment, his teeth nibbling the soft skin at the inside of her thighs, his sharp, darting tongue creating both havoc and bliss to her shattered senses. Her eyes brimmed with tears at the tumultuous pleasure he was giving her.

"Jan?" Dave stopped, capturing her chin in his fingers so he could look into her eyes. "Are you all right, honey?"

She could only nod, the wobbly smile and liquid sheen of her brilliant green eyes attempting to assure him there was nothing wrong. Indeed, at this moment—for the first time in so very long—everything was perfect. Absolutely, heavenly perfect.

His eyes still held a shadow of doubt and Jan shook her head, extricating herself from his embrace to rise up on her knees. She bent over him, her fingers running little trails down the soft, red-gold curls of his chest. She found the dark buttons buried deep within and bent her head, her lips encircling them and drawing at them with her flicking tongue until she heard his husky moans and saw the fires flare a little higher in the smoldering depths of his eyes.

Her fingers slid over the firm muscles of his stomach, delighting in the feel of his body arching against her touch as she slowly made her way downward, bliss just a touch away. Jan grew bolder, marveling that she could give this glorious man such obvious pleasure. Surely this was making love. This sharing of the gift. Each person giving and taking of the ecstasy. She felt a warmth inside her for Dave Barrie that threatened to overwhelm her at any moment.

"Oh, Jan . . . what have you done to me?" Dave groaned and pulled her onto him, fitting her curves to his hard male length. "Oh, babe . . . I'd given up thinking you existed."

The feel of his body under hers was driving Jan to sheer desperation and she molded herself against him, wanting more. Nothing but total possession would satisfy the fires raging through her veins, fires that had turned her blood to a torrent of molten, churning gold.

His arms clamped like iron bands as he rolled over, bringing her with him, his hand moving down her body, massaging fingers preparing her for him with a gentle, sensuous touch.

"Oh, Dave," she breathed, moving into the delicate caresses, "please. I want you to love me. I want you so much."

"Not as much as I've wanted you, Jan," he growled against her lips as he pulled her to him, fitting himself between her thighs as if they'd been created by a master sculptor to mold together in just this way.

Her lips curled around his seeking, probing tongue while she arched toward him with sheer feminine pleasure as he completed the rapturous union. Jan's hips moved sinuously against him, her hands roaming down the muscled hardness of his back to grasp the firm buttocks, pulling him deeper into her feminine warmth with an innate seductiveness that would have shocked her at any other time.

She clasped hold of him as her body rose and fell to his deep, thrusting strokes, feeling the rising urgency surging forth from her very core. His hands moved under her, lifting and molding her to him. She cried out, her fingers curving like talons, clutching his shoulders as she exploded into a cataclysmic fireball. Dave was only an instant behind, holding her tightly against him, kissing away the salty tears that were pouring from her eyes.

"It's all right, Jan. It's better than all right. It's terrific, sweetheart."

"Oh, Dave," she whispered, her face soft and vulnerable. "I was so frightened for a moment. I've never felt like that before."

"I know." He brushed back her hair from her face, looping dark glossy strands around her ear. "It's a first for both of us, Jan. Absolutely incredible. You're incredible."

He held her close into the curve of his arm, bestowing soft, gentle kisses on her hair as their hands feathered over each other's bodies, no longer in hunger, but in sweet memory. Jan drifted into a light sleep, to be awakened later in the night by the soft cloud of breath at her throat. She turned in his arms, eager for his renewed embrace.

By the time the blazing desert sun was streaming into the room through the part in the heavy draperies, Jan and Dave had learned each other well. There was nothing he didn't know about her tanned, responsive female body. No secrets had been withheld as he'd stroked and coaxed her to the euphoric heights of ecstasy.

In return, he'd held nothing back, urging Jan's tentative, exploring fingers and lips to grow more intrepid, learning to read his needs and desires as a blind man would read braille.

They knew everything about each other—yet they knew nothing.

Jan rolled over, inhaling the warm, musky scent of him as her cheek grazed the empty pillow. She leaned up on her elbow, gazing about the room. He was gone. But her perusing study took in the watch on the dresser and the masculine clothing still scat-

tered about the floor. Wherever Dave Barrie was, he
was definitely returning.

She rose reluctantly from the tangled sheets, not
wanting to forsake the warmth and the aroma that
was a mixture of him, her, and—the best part—the
sweet redolence of their lovemaking. She walked
over to read a note he'd propped up on the table,
her lean, stretched muscles unusually stiff and sore
this morning.

Written on a small notepad with an unmistak-
able television-network logo in the corner, it read:

> I never did buy dinner. Will you settle for
> breakfast this morning and dinner the rest of
> our lives? You deserve champagne and caviar,
> sweetheart, but I suspect the best I'm going to
> do at the motel coffeeshop is coffee and donuts.
> Keep the bed warm.
>
>   Love, Dave.

Jan slumped down on the edge of the bed, rubbing her fingers across her eyes until she could see
dancing stars on a background of black velvet.
What in the world had she done? Spent the entire
night with a man whose name she hadn't even
known until minutes before he was making passionate love to her. And she to him.

No, she corrected firmly, not love. It had been a
wild, purely physical night of desire. At the time,
everything had seemed brushed with a romantic,
golden glow, but in the bright light of day Jan saw her
wanton behavior as cheap. And decidedly sickening.

She threw on her dress, stepped into the bikini
panties and sandals, and ran her fingers through
her hair with hurried strokes. Then she grabbed her
purse and moved to the door. Opening it cautiously,
Jan didn't see anyone moving across the wide
asphalt parking lot. She ran to her car and gunned
the engine to life, driving away from the Three
Palms Motel as if pursued by the devil himself.

Chapter Three

Three weeks after that extraordinary night, David Matthew Barrie, more easily recognized by network news viewers as Dave Barrie, had just wrapped up an interview with the San Diego Chief of Police. Pleased with the way it had gone, he went to supervise the editing before it ran on the six-o'clock news. He watched as the tape editor did his magic, managing to compact the twenty-minute conversation into three concise minutes of news.

"It's going to be great stuff, Dave," Kenny Wilkens said as he ran the videotape through the monitor. "But what's new, huh? The stuff you give me a six-year-old could edit into brilliance."

Dave grinned, shaking his head. "You get half the credit, Ken. I'm just grateful KNET has someone with your talents. It could be a frustrating few weeks, otherwise."

Dave Barrie had a reputation for never doing anything in halfway measures. He drove himself to the fullest, and more than one disgruntled associate had discovered that his easygoing exterior cloaked a core of pure steel.

He'd bought a cup of thick, bitter coffee from the machine and was idly chewing on the cardboard rim of the cup, watching the rest of the news tapes receive their final cuts. His wandering blue gaze slid over to a tape being wound next to his and he suddenly looked as if he'd been hit with a two-by-four in the gut.

"Who's that?" His sharp bark would have done justice to a mastiff.

"Who?" The young film editor running the segment looked up, her eyes widening as she viewed the intense stare radiating from his eyes.

"That woman! Who is she?"

Jackson Cullen, sportscaster for KNET, glanced up. "That's Jan Baxter," he remarked.

Dave's eyes skimmed over the figure clad in the red tank suit. Designed for speed in the water, the competition suits had become incredibly thin, allowing none of Jan's firm body to escape his study. But he didn't need this opportunity to observe that figure. He'd known every square inch of it backward and forward before she'd disappeared from his motel room that morning.

"Why the film clip?" he asked with an outward calm that surprised himself.

Jackson Cullen shrugged carelessly. "She's the diving coach over in La Jolla. La Conquista Swimming and Diving Club. Seems she's brought in a new kid to train. A real Olympic contender, according to the scuttlebutt around the water-logged circles."

Blue eyes were still locked on the red-suited figure on the small screen. "Is the kid from Phoenix?"

"Yeah." Jackson Cullen turned to look at him with interest. "How'd you know that?"

"Lucky guess," Dave muttered, his lips thinning as he raked his long fingers through the crisp ginger hair. "Baxter . . . the name rings a bell."

"That figures. She won a silver medal in the seventy-two Olympics in Munich. The whole thing was kind of overshadowed by the terrorist deal, but there were those who swore the girl could fly when she came off that high platform."

Dave crushed the cardboard cup in his hand, his brow furrowed in thought. "Now I remember. There was some problem, wasn't there? Something to do with illegal drugs?"

The sportscaster laughed off the inquiry. "Boy, you're really getting into that sports-and-drug story, aren't you? If you're going to go back that far, you'll need every hour the network has scheduled for news coverage for the next ten years." The voice grew serious. "But in answer to your question, Jan got a bad rap. Her doctor had changed some asthma medication and her coach thought it was on the approved list. Since it was discovered in the pretrials, the entire deal was cleared up in time for her to participate in the games."

"I've got your clip ready, Dave. Want to monitor it?"

"Yeah, just a sec, Ken. Hey, Cullen, where is this La Conquista?"

With the instructions in his pocket and the police tape finished to his satisfaction, Dave Barrie left the studio, cramming his long frame into the interior of his BMW, and headed up the coast.

Jan, who had only ever seen him smiling, wouldn't have recognized the hard set to his features.

She watched the last of her students trudging from the showers, promising to be back by six-thirty the following morning. It was a long, wearying life, as much for the coach as it was the young divers. They were all chasing that elusive medal that never promised to bring fame or fortune. Or, heaven knows, happiness. Just a fleeting mention in the sports archives and the inner satisfaction that comes with knowing you've done your best.

Jan was especially tired today. She'd spent the major part of the afternoon dodging unwanted attention from the president of the club, James Waring III. Not only president of this athletic club, the man was an officer of several others that were even more exclusive. He was on the board of a prestigious bank and was married to a descendant of one of San Diego's first families. Waring was also the father of two teenagers, both of whom were on her diving team. The older one showed every sign of following in his father's footsteps—in more ways than one.

For James Waring III was, first and foremost, an unprincipled womanizer. And one of the most persistent types at that. They'd had angry words when he'd first attempted to use his leverage as the newly elected president against her stalwart refusals. These days, they'd settled into an unpleasant routine of more subtle feints and parries. Though Jan had discovered she could handle the man, the effort proved incredibly tiring at times. She stretched, rubbing the back of her neck and rotating her head in lazy circles. Then she did the only thing she knew to do for stress.

Executing a perfect dive from the side of the pool, she began swimming long, strenuous laps, determined to work out the tension that held such a tight grip on her.

She was doing a flip turn in the deep end when a long shadow appeared over the water and she turned to look up at its source. Her face went as white as the plaster coating of the pool and she dived down quickly to the bottom, saying any number of small, frantic prayers on her way back up.

"You can't stay down there all night. Not without a snorkle." Crystal-blue eyes observed her blandly.

"What are you doing here?" Jan sputtered,

coughing out some of the water she'd swallowed in her shock. She tred water, her head tilting back to look into Dave's implacable face.

"I think we've got this interview out of sequence," he said, coming to squat down on the cantilevered decking, apparently not caring that his expensive loafers were in a puddle of water. "The key question is, what are *you* doing here? Do you have any idea how many Bannings there are in Tucson?"

As her green eyes flashed with guilt, he nodded grimly. "Oh, yes, I went there as soon as magical Marvin finished repairing the car. He, by the way, took the same attitude as you. Anyone with enough money to own a sporty little import like that should be able to pay through the nose for parts. I could've built my first fifty-seven Ford from scratch with what I laid out for two belts and a filter."

Dave gave her a droll grin, and in the late-afternoon sunlight she watched the lines deepen around his eyes.

"Marvin," he continued, "has a Robin Hood complex. He works on foreign cars so he can rob from the rich and feed the poor. These days, however, Marvin is eating a lot better than I am."

His deep chuckle relieved the tension that had strung between them, and Jan marveled, in spite of her shock, at this man who could laugh so easily at himself.

"Are you going to stay in the water forever, or come up here? I'd like to talk to you man to woman instead of man to dolphin."

Jan put her hands on the decking, levering herself up and out of the pool to sit beside his increasingly wet feet. The water ran off her smooth body, puddling around them.

"Your shoes are getting soaked."

"Seem to be." His eyes, however, continued their study of her face.

"Did you really try to call me in Tucson?"

"Call you?" Dave gave her a faintly censorious glance. "Who said anything about calling? I didn't call you. I drove there and looked up every single Banning listed and showed up on their doorsteps. There's quite a lot of them, in case you didn't know. And, to a Banning uncle, they think I'm an escaped mental patient. Including one very brawny construction worker with arms the size of Virginia hams who threatened me with severe bodily harm if I ever came near his wife again." His lips quirked. "Do you think it hurts to have your lung kicked out?"

"His wife?" Jan's eyes were huge green circles.

There were sparks of humor in his. "Yep. Scared the living daylights out of me for a minute. Oh, I wasn't going to give you up, you understand. Not on your life! Or mine, as it may have turned out. This guy, honey, was a mountain."

"But not my husband."

He grinned, pushing her wet, disordered hair off her creased forehead. "No. Fortunately, I discovered that before I wound up in the Tucson hospital encased in a plaster body cast, minus one lung. *His* Jan Banning had long red hair, a slightly plump but still voluptuous figure, and a glint in those hazel eyes which gave me the distinct impression that her hubby had been through that routine before."

Jan's feet hung in the water, her toes trailing rippling circles as she looked up at the teasing blue eyes. "You went to all that trouble? Why?"

Dave took her chin in his long fingers and held her head so she couldn't turn away. "If you don't know that, Jan Banning Baxter," he warned softly, "you're not nearly the woman I've already credited you with being." His keen gaze softened, the dark blue rims on the outside of his irises flaring as his thumbs traced the outline of her mouth.

"Your pants are getting wet now."

"Damn the pants." The intense look didn't flicker.

"Who are you?" Jan asked on a shaky, ragged breath.

"You already know that. I'm Dave Barrie and you also know everything about me that's important. Anything else can be related to you by my mother, who will only tell you what a sweet, endearing boy I am. But you've already discovered that for yourself."

He tipped forward in his squatting position, rocking on the balls of his feet to place a quick kiss on the lips he'd just touched.

"Now, get that firm little butt into the locker room. We're going to dinner."

"I'm not going to dinner with you!"

Wonderful blue eyes narrowed. "I owe you one, Jan. And I'm a man of my word. Go get ready."

His easygoing tone was like steel wrapped in silk, and Jan realized he'd brook no argument on the issue. As he released her, she rose and marched defiantly to the locker room, determined not to let him see her fear.

Dave stood, arms folded across his chest as he watched the steely spine and the smooth rhythm of her hips. Jan could feel his steady male appraisal, and although he'd seen her in less, she had never felt more naked in her life.

She ran the shower as cold as she could stand, lifting her face to the stinging needles, trying to prick some sense into her head. What in the world was she going to do? When she'd awakened that morning in Phoenix, she could feel only shame for what must have been a bad reaction to her thirtieth birthday. Nothing more.

But since that passion-filled night, instead of having relieved the tensions, the incident had made her even jumpier, as if her skin had been deprived of some calming substance in the air. She'd been unable to get the tall, ginger-haired man from her mind. And now, having him show up here only proved that her judgment had been way off. She never should have stopped the car that day. Dave Barrie *was* a dangerous man!

"You going to stay in here all night?"

Jan's troubled green eyes flew up to the long body lounging in the doorway, holding a towel. She bent, instinctively protective.

"Dave! This is the women's locker room!"

"No one's here."

"But it's a public place."

He shook his tawny head, the crooked smile not leaving his lips. "Not really. It's a private club."

"But there are still other people who could come along."

"Nope. They're all gone. I watched them close up and leave. Want some help getting that hard-to-reach spot in the middle of your back?"

"No!"

"I can remember when you liked sharing a shower with me." His blue eyes appeared wounded, but his mouth still quirked in a teasing, warm grin.

Yes, she'd loved the feel of his hands lathering her body, moving across her heated skin in seductive circles, cleansing her of anyone who might have hoped to hold a candle to Dave Barrie in her memory. That had been only one of his ideas that night, each becoming more and more scintillating until he'd won the contest—and her heart—hands down.

Now Jan could only watch in shock as he pulled off the narrow brown tie and slipped it into the pocket of his dark-blue jacket. Shrugging off the jacket, Dave laid it carefully and deliberately on the stack of white towels and began to slowly unbutton the crisp tan shirt, his laughing eyes teasing her with each freed button. The shirt joined the jacket and Jan's eyes rested on the reddish-gold hairs, following them as they arrowed down to disappear below his belt line. Her fingertips tingled with memory and she experienced a slight shiver.

"I'd say you're getting cold in there all alone." His keen gaze hadn't missed her shudder. "I'll come scrub your back and keep you nice and warm."

Dave's hands moved suggestively to the narrow waistband and Jan straightened up, common sense overruling her mutinous body, which was right now straining for his touch.

"No! I'll get out. Just hand me that towel, will you?"

"Come and get it."

Her hand was outstretched, her green eyes softly pleading. Jan generally disdained such overt, feminine ploys, but with this man she knew she'd have to use every weapon in her arsenal.

She could tell that Dave wasn't immune to the soulful gaze, but she watched with fascinated interest as he drew himself even taller, waving the towel slightly. He grinned provocatively, appearing to leash every memory of the night they'd shared together.

"Good try. I love that look! It's incredible sexy, darlin'. But it's your choice. You come to me, or I come to you. And to give you fair warning, if I join you under that water, you're going to end up on the blue ceramic tile floor while I love you until neither one of us can move. Which would result in the need for a bit of explaining in the morning when those kids show up and find their coach in the arms of a blissfully satiated man."

The smile hadn't faded one little bit, but there was a deep streak of cold steel in his eyes that let Jan know she'd met her match. For now, anyway. She sighed, turned off the water, and walked toward him. Jan held out her arms as she allowed him to wrap her in the fleecy folds of the towel and draw her to him.

"Now, isn't this nice and cozy?" he asked, his hands rubbing her back, drying her skin under the soft white terry cloth.

"Dave, I—"

"I'm trying my damnedest to be a good sport about this entire farce, Jan," he warned, his deep voice becoming suddenly gruff. She thought she caught the slightest tinge of a drawl, but his next words made the thought escape her mind entirely.

"I'm not exactly sure what little game you've been playing, but I only want to know one thing right now. Are you married?"

Relief flooded her face. She could handle that one. "No."

Keen blue eyes studied her appraisingly. "Truth this time?"

Jan nodded, her own eyes directed at a spot down at their feet, where the water was dripping onto his shoes again. They were definitely going to be ruined. "Truth," she answered softly.

"Good." Dave backed away from her, slipping his shirt back on. He undid the slacks, sliding the zipper all the way down in order to tuck the shirt back in.

"Dave?" Jan couldn't take her eyes from the gesture, her mind bringing forth the erotic memories.

He had followed her line of vision, satisfied sparks of humor in his gaze. "What is it, darlin'?"

Jan yanked her eyes back to his face, not finding a great deal of relief there as he regarded her with unnerving warmth. "What would you have said if I *was* married?"

"It wouldn't have made a bit of difference, Jan. We both know I staked my claim to Jan Banning Baxter in Phoenix and it's irrevocable. It just would've made things a bit messier if you had a husband out there somewhere." He ignored her slight gasp. "I've got to get back to work. But I'll pick you up about seven. Are you going to give me your address, or do I have to start harassing all the Baxters in San Diego the same way I did the Bannings in Tucson? This could end up getting me killed, woman!"

"Five seventy-four Oceancrest Drive," she answered. "It's across the bay on Coronado Island."

"Make it a bit after seven," he decided. "And be hungry. For food. I swear we'll take care of that first tonight. Scout's honor."

He held up his right hand in the gesture of a pledge and Jan knew, despite his wide smile, that this was no Boy Scout standing in the doorway. The man had the capacity to sweep all coherent thought from her mind with a single glance, a mere touch. He was intoxicating, beguiling, and dangerous. So incredibly dangerous.

"Dave," Jan's voice was a trembling whisper. "How did you find me?"

He turned his wrist, frowning as he eyed his watch. "Long story, sweetheart, and I don't have the time right now. Tell you what—you watch the six-o'clock news on Channel Seven and I'll explain everything tonight. O.K.?"

Jan tugged the towel around her now-dry body, her slanted green eyes wide and confused, like a cat caught in the beam of a headlight.

"O.K.," she murmured, watching his long,

loping gait as he left the locker room and ran for the parking lot.

"Oh, my God!" Maggie gasped, her brown eyes as wide as a stunned doe's. Jan continued to relate the entire incident, up through the locker room, to her best friend. "And now he's *here? In* San Diego?" She'd begun mixing the margaritas at the beginning of the story and now poured them, handing one to Jan.

Jan licked some of the crystal salt from the rim of the glass, answering the question with a bleak nod.

"Why is he here, do you suppose?" her friend mused aloud.

Jan shook her head, running her fingers through the sleek straight line of her dark hair. "I don't know. He said he'd tell me later and told me to watch the news."

"A mystery man!" Maggie beamed with vicarious excitement. "You lucky girl. This is frightfully romantic."

Jan opened her mouth to give Maggie a wry answer when the news came on to the already lit screen. She leaned forward to turn up the sound. The two women—one tall and dark-haired; the other petite and blond, best friends since childhood—watched obediently. Two pairs of eyes followed the latest Middle East crisis, learned of the president's newest strategy in the economic war, and viewed the mayor cutting a red ribbon to open the first in a chain of vegetarian taco stands.

Then they watched a pair of athletes trading insults over beer, and a commercial for a new, improved miracle detergent, Beyond, that was guaranteed to whiten clothes beyond white. Still there was no clue to Jan's mystery man as Maggie was gleefully calling him.

"Oh, look, there you are!" Maggie clapped her hands as Jan's interview with Jackson Cullen aired.

A prickling of fear raised the short hairs on the back of Jan's neck. She'd met her "mystery man" in Phoenix on the trip to see Jimmy Cassidy. A frown skittered across her puckered brow as she sought to put the pieces together.

"Maggie! That's him!"

Jan turned as snowy as a sheet washed in Beyond as she pointed with a trembling finger toward the screen.

Maggie could only eye her incredulously. "Dave Barrie? *He's* your mystery man?"

Jan nodded, the huge lump that had taken residence in her throat preventing even an answering squawk.

"Why didn't you tell me it was Dave Barrie?" Maggie's astonished gaze moved back and forth between the compelling male figure on the screen and her friend, whose taut body was bent in an angle aimed toward the television set.

Jan drank in the smooth, controlled tones of the deep baritone voice, but what she was hearing was most definitely not an interview with the police chief. No, she could hear that velvet voice crooning words of love and desire into her burning ears. Words that no man had ever said to Jan Baxter. Words that she had never wanted a man to say to her. Until now.

Maggie rose to turn off the set when he'd disappeared into the rolling credits. "Ok, kiddo. Let's have have the entire story this time. You spent one blissful day and one glorious night of passionate, unrestrained ecstasy with Dave Barrie and you didn't *tell* me?"

"I didn't realize you'd know him."

Maggie expelled an exasperated breath. "Didn't you?"

Jan shook her head. "Uh uh. Should I have?"

"Don't you ever watch television?"

"Not the evening news. I'm usually working. I read the paper, though," she added, feeling a need to defend her awareness of current world events. She might not have recognized Dave Barrie on sight, but she was no dummy.

"Well, didn't you talk about what he did for a living?"

An attractive deep rose filled the skin under Jan's tan. That explained the memo pad with the network logo. She'd been so distraught that morning, she'd never given it a second thought.

"We didn't—uh—get around to that."

"I'll bet not."

"All right, Maggie. You know a secret I don't. Give."

Jan poured the last of the margaritas into their glasses and sat back, crossing her long legs in a fluid, graceful movement, and waited.

"Well, he's been a network foreign correspondent for ages. And he's either followed around by a little cloud of disaster that hovers obediently over his head, or he's incredibly lucky. Or he's a hell of a bloodhound. At any rate, he's always right on top of a fast-breaking story."

Jan thought about how his car just happened to break down on the day she was uncharacteristically driving to Phoenix. And how he just happened to be staying at a motel right around the corner from the pool where the meet had been held. And how, after turning Tucson upside down searching for her, she popped up in his very own newsroom.

"All three, I'd guess," she offered. She turned distressed jade eyes toward her friend. "But what's he doing here in San Diego?"

"Well," Maggie said, her expression taking on the smug look she'd worn as a kid whenever she'd manage to squeak one step ahead of Jan, "there's a number of conjectures." She began ticking them off on long, peach-tinted fingernails.

"*Newsworld* magazine reports he's tired of traveling the world like a video gypsy and has decided to settle down for a time doing local broadcasts in the lovely Mediterranean climate of our fair city. They also intimated that he's making a power play in order to force the network into giving him an evening anchor position.

"*Celebrity* magazine insists he left Europe after a knockdown, drag-out brawl with his latest mistress, an Italian soprano. And"—she bent down a third finger—"*Inside Scoop*, that tabloid known for its less-than-subtle gossip, says he managed to infiltrate his way into an oil sheikh's harem in Saudi Arabia. And that it was only through delicate negotiations by the U.S. State Department that he was allowed to choose deportation, instead of beheading. It's also rumored that they expect an unusual number of little tawny-haired princes and princesses to be born in a certain remote desert sheikhdom next spring."

"For heaven's sake, Maggie," Jan retorted, "you make him sound like a combination of Valentino, Ali Khan, and . . . and . . ." She struggled to come up with a modern-day sex symbol to equal the first two, "Tom Selleck!" Not exactly hitting the nail directly on the head, but close enough to get her idea across. "He's attractive, granted, but he's no Greek god."

"You, my friend, are a dodo. Or is it an ostrich? That silly bird who sticks his head in the sand? Well, at any rate, you're certainly one odd duck if you don't recognize the single most important element of sex appeal."

"And that is?" Jan arched a delicate, dark brow.

"Power! Kissinger was no Greek god, either,"

Maggie pointed out. "But remember all those gorgeous actresses willing to claw each other's contact lenses out for a chance to sit next to the man at a White House dinner?" She shook her finger in Jan's face. "Power is the world's oldest, most proven aphrodisiac!"

"And Dave Barrie has power?" Jan thought of the sweet, gentle man with the laughing blue eyes. The man who'd held her in his arms on that ridiculous merry-go-round horse, kicking his heels into the wooden sides and flicking the reins, urging it forward. Power?

Then she remembered his calm but effective refusal to allow her escape this afternoon. The man with the concealed sharp edges under his smooth surface. Power? Perhaps.

"Maggie," she asked, "if he's as important as you say, Dave would've had to survive a lot of network infighting, wouldn't he? And manipulated quite a few of his own?"

"Sure, hon. Why?"

She followed Jan's gaze to the forest-green car that was pulling up outside the front window.

"Because," Jan sighed, wrenching her gaze away from the car and rubbing her hands on her white clamdiggers as she moved toward the door, "I think this time I may have just dived in over my head."

Chapter Four

"You didn't run away." Dave Barrie's bright eyes caressed Jan's face with such intimacy as she let him in that she felt her toes curling into the soft, grass-green carpeting. Maggie had deserted her, escaping out the back door, apparently deciding that discretion was the better part of valor.

"Could I have gotten away this time?"

"No," he answered with an air of unshakable self-confidence. "Not this time, Jan."

A strained silence settled into the room, like misty, early-morning fog.

"Am I really that hard to take?" he finally asked.

"Why do you ask that?" Her green eyes met his disappointed gaze.

"You're clenching that poor, chapped lower lip between your teeth." He drew nearer, his finger tracing a line along her lip, which was unconsciously captured in a tight, nervous bite.

It wasn't safe to think when the man was around! But that night in Phoenix showed what could happen when Jan allowed her heart to rule her head. He created a dynamic assault to her senses, like a deep whiff of straight chlorine.

"Don't be silly." Jan laughed unsteadily. Then, seeking to detour the subject, she asked, "And haven't any of your women friends ever advised you not to refer to a lady's lips as poor? Or chapped? They're suppose to be sweeter than wine. Honey. Soft as spun silk. You must be slipping, now that you've returned to the provinces, Mr. Barrie. Contrary to what you may have heard about the new, liberated American female, we happen to like romance every bit as much as our European sisters."

An impish light glowed in his blue eyes, drawing and holding Jan's attention as she felt herself falling under his hypnotic spell. She knew she'd walked right into *that* one! Trying to outthink this man was like going head to head with a high-speed computer. She was licked before she even began.

"I'm sorry," his deep voice curled over her. "But it's nice to know. I was getting the distinct impression that romantic involvement was exactly what you were dodging. I'll begin making amends right now."

Dave reached deep into his pocket and extracted a slim tube. Pulling off the small white cap, he caught her chin between his thumb and forefinger and lifted her expectant face. The steady hand moved the Chapstick across her softly parted lips, bringing back a flood of sensual memories that threatened to drown her. Why should such a simple gesture suddenly seem so incredibly intimate?

Jan ran her tongue over her lips. No flavor. Trust Dave to prefer the simple kind. No orange, cherry, or spicy mint. Just plain, honest Chapstick. *Honest Chapstick?* Good Lord, she was going bonkers. Certifiably insane. It would only be a matter of time before the men in the white coats arrived to drag her away. Obviously, Jan decided grimly, your brain deteriorates at thirty, leaving your body to function on its own. Which, she'd already discovered, is a horrendous mistake.

"There." The tube disappeared back into the pockets of the slim dress slacks and he seemed unaware of the fleeting havoc he'd just subjected her to. His lips touched hers in a brief, much-too-short peck. "Does that make you feel any better about me?"

Better? If the man made her feel any better, he'd be illegal! Knowing enough not to be quite so honest, Jan nodded silently and granted him a wobbly smile.

"Ready to go? If you feel like fish, we can try Anthony's. But, just name it."

Jan cast a glance down at her white cotton clamdiggers and buttercup-yellow halter top. She'd been so wound up since arriving home, she'd forgotten to change.

"Oh, Dave, I'm sorry," she apologized. "I'm not dressed—"

His blue eyes were definitely admiring. "No problem." He loosened his knit tie, pulling it off and jamming it into his pocket with a look of heartfelt relief. He took her hand and led her to the door. "I think you look terrific just the way you are. And don't worry, I happen to be a fair-to-middlin' cook."

Jan skidded to a stop. "We're going to your place?" Damn! Her voice had risen on the end of that question high enough to shatter glass. She sounded like a seventeen-year-old on her first day in the big city.

"Scared?" There was a teasing, challenging light in the eyes watching her from beneath arched brows.

"Of course not. I *am* grown up, Dave Barrie," Jan said briskly, squaring her slim shoulders.

"And you did it so well, too," he murmured, measuring her slender curves with a practiced eye.

Dave pulled the BMW up in front of a tall apartment building on Mission Bay, giving the keys to a uniformed young man who slid behind the wheel as they walked toward the door. There was a disconcerting grinding of gears and a loud roar from the intricately tuned engine as the attendant pulled the car out of the curving drive.

"So much for jeweled action and surgical gearbox accuracy." He grinned down at her, sounding as if he were quoting the owner's manual. "The kid's new."

"He'll be gone soon, if he keeps that up," Jan observed, wondering how many other occupants of this building would be so nonchalant about the careless handling of their expensive cars.

He put his hand lightly on her back, guiding her into the luxurious building. They were quiet on the short ride in the modern elevator, the trip so fast that Jan feared she'd left her stomach on the first floor as it lurched to a stop. She glanced up, noting that the orange-lit numbers indicated they were on the top floor. Still with his hand casually on her back, Dave led her down a long hallway, carpeted in soft, plush, ice-blue, to a set of double doors at the end of the quiet hall. Opening the door, he ushered her in with a flourish.

Pressing a silent switch, Dave lit the room to a dim, iridescent glow. It was difficult to tell just where the penthouse apartment left off and the San Diego skyline began. They were high above Mission Bay and Jan could see the moon glistening on the water through an entire wall of glass. Mirrored walls and silver vertical blinds reflected the view in all directions, as if bathing them in a gleaming metallic womb. The floors were tiled, the color of creamy white fudge, topped in places by furry shell-white area rugs. The upholstery was a stark hue of alabaster, draped tightly to mold the furniture into hard, sleek lines. Glass and silver predominated, giving almost an operating-room sterility to the admittedly luxurious apartment.

"Like it?" His face was impassive as he studied her expression in the muted light.

"Truth?"

Dave nodded. "Truth."

Jan walked over to the glass, gazing down at the foamy whitecaps on the bay and the smooth shining ripples lapping onto gold sand.

"I love the view. Would you ever believe this used to be a swampy old mudflat?"

Dave crossed the expanse of white flooring to stand behind her, his fingers slipping around her waist as he pulled her back against the hard wall of his chest.

"The lady likes the view," he murmured, his lips so close to her ear that she could feel his sweet breath warming her skin. "But how does the lady like the apartment?" he persisted.

Darn. What could she say? It was obvious that a great deal of money had been poured into some very elaborate decorating. It was also obvious that the place held absolutely no personality except that of the absent decorator. But, once burned, Dave Barrie would be on his toes. He'd spot a lie from her a mile off.

"I hate it."

Dave gave her a fond squeeze, leaning down to feather a series of exotic little kisses across the back of her neck.

"I knew you would," he answered, his lips plucking her tender skin. There was a strange air of satisfaction in his tone. "So do I."

Jan turned around, her green gaze widening as she searched his face. The reflected lights of the room caught in the blue eyes as those familiar lines fanned out.

"It's not my place," he explained. "I'm just staying here temporarily. It belongs to the network. They call it a hospitality suite." His grin tilted devilishly. "If you think this room is something, you should see the bedroom. I've got a sneaking suspicion that the type of hospitality usually offered around here isn't just cocktails and canapés."

Was that an invitation? A proposition? Jan couldn't tell. Nervously. she slid out of his light embrace and walked back to the center of the huge room, gazing with apparent interest at a black onyx statue of a well-endowed female nude.

"They let you stay here? Just like that?"

"Until I find a place. I've just been too busy to look."

Jan looked around, taking in the aura of the stark apartment. Tall vases were filled with fresh hothouse flowers and she had a hunch that Dave didn't bother himself with trimming stems and replacing wilted blossoms. A housekeeper obviously came in every day. All this. And Maggie's declaration that Jan was probably the only person on earth who wouldn't recognize the man in a dark alley.

"You're pretty important to the network, aren't you?" It was asked quietly, and she already knew the answer.

Dave responded easily, without false humility. "Yes, I suppose I am."

She ran her finger along the slanted shoulder of the onyx statue, phrasing the next question over and over in her mind. With the patience of a born interviewer, Dave waited, giving her time.

"And you probably think I'm incredibly stupid."

Shock paled his friendly face for an instant and Jan lifted her gaze to observe him carefully, noting for the first time a sprinkling of freckles across the broken ridge of his nose. Faint little bits of color that were usually hidden under his tan.

"Stupid?" His voice sounded as though it was forced. It had an unusual quality, rough and gravelly. "Where in the world did you come up with that idea?"

"I didn't recognize you," she murmured to the silent stone woman.

Dave took her hand and led Jan to the sofa, turning toward her as he sat down, his arm stretched along the top. "And do you have any idea what a sublime pleasure that was—once I believed it?" His low voice vibrated slightly as he reached out and lifted her downcast gaze to his. Soft blue eyes caressed her lovingly.

"When I first got into your car and you lit into me the way you did," he continued, "I was stunned. I mean, I'm used to women coming up with original opening gambits, but I'd never run into one who attacked at first sight. Then, the next day, I began to suspect you really didn't know who I was. But, without meaning to sound disgustingly vain"—the fine network of lines at the corners of his eyes deepened, along with the grooves on either side of his mouth—"I didn't see how that was possible."

"Unless I'd spent the past years on the moon."

Dave nodded, his smile giving him an incredibly boyish look. "And if you had, it's a cinch I would've been there covering the event. So, you still would have known me."

"Then—"

Dave held up a hand. "Wait a minute and let me finish," he instructed in the tone of a man comfortable with getting his way. "When you stood there, so heartbreakingly lovely, with those green eyes as soft and inviting as a tropical lagoon, and asked me who you'd just won, I could tell you weren't playing some game. It was like you'd lifted ten tons from my shoulders."

"How?" Jan searched his face, meeting only gentle amusement in his steady, friendly eyes.

"It had been a very long time since I'd been alone with a woman. Usually there's the woman, me, and my reputation." He grinned wickedly. "A reputation which would've been blown to smithereens if I'd let the kid in me come out to play like I did with you. A kid, by the way, who'd never been fortunate enough to run free in an amusement park like we did together." His face grew shuttered for a moment, dark shades hiding any emotion in his blue eyes, but she could see the muscles of his jaw clenching at some distant memory.

As fast as the tension appeared, it vanished, and Dave was smiling again.

"Do you have any idea," he asked, his voice revealing nothing of the brief bitterness she'd thought she'd seen, "how terrifying it is to feel you have to live up to some inflated idea of supermasculine performance? It wreaks havoc on the male ego."

Jan shivered with emotion, recalling with vivid detail their night together. "I don't think you'd ever have to worry about your male ego," she murmured.

He shook his ginger head. "Ah, there's where you're dead wrong, babe. We all have delicate egos. Even, it appears, beautiful, desirable women who refuse to take a man's heartfelt admiration seriously."

"Dave—" Jan turned her head away, intent on the stunning view outside the wall of glass.

"Why do I make you so nervous and unhappy?" His long fingers stroked the back of her hand, as if soothing a nervous Thoroughbred. "I can remember you enjoying our time together. I know you weren't acting, Jan. I know you're not the type of lady who usually indulges in such uninhibited romps."

"You're right about that," she muttered.

"Canoeing? You don't usually do that, do you?"

"No."

"And frolics through Kiddyland? None of that frivolous stuff?"

"No." Jan's voice mirrored her regret at that one.

"And picking up strange men with broken-down foreign cars along desert highways. I'll bet that's not a usual exploit for Jan Baxter, either."

She was grateful for the dim lighting, which hid the hot flush rising from her chest to spread over her face. "No, that was a first."

"I'm glad." The voice was low and soft and vibrated with a slight tremor of emotion.

Jan turned back to gaze into his blue eyes, which had moved closer. "Why?" It was a whisper.

"I'm glad I was the first for you, Jan," he said simply.

Surely he knew. With all his experience . . . "Dave, I'm thirty years old. I've been married; you . . ." She closed her eyes and took a deep breath, praying for strength. "You weren't the first."

The dark cloud that had been covering the crescent moon drifted out to sea, and moonlight streamed into the room like silent, silvery dust to expose the open and incredibly tender look he was giving her.

"Yes I was," Dave insisted quietly, but firmly. "I was in all the ways that could possibly ever count. As you were with me."

Her glossy dark hair curved under her chin in a smooth line and his fingers played with it as he brushed the strands back from her face. Looping them around her ear, he nibbled lightly on the soft skin of her lobe and the tiny sensation of pain was oddly, satisfyingly, stimulating.

"Every way," he murmured, his knuckles tracing a soft path down her cheekbone, along her slender throat. His fingers splayed over her skin, his thumb resting on her skipping pulse as he pulled her to the kiss that was coming.

As his tawny ginger head lowered, Jan realized that restraint wasn't necessary. Once again she was succumbing to that odd sensuality that Dave's inexhaustible confidence about their relationship instilled. He was so certain of success, so positive of the outcome, that he almost had her believing it herself.

But Jan Baxter was made of sterner stuff than that. She was an expert in self-discipline, having subscribed to it all her life. It flowed through her veins right along with her blood. It had been necessary, in order to turn her back on all the carefree, delightful things that childhood offers to the average youngster. It had been required of her to reject the exciting, tumultuous experiences of adolescence, choosing a shelf full of trophies over homecoming games and spring proms. It had been that self-discipline which had been rewarded by an Olympic medal, and that same strength had become an intrinsic part of her.

Jan knew that this time she'd be able to control things. Her behavior in Phoenix had led to a strange, aberrant experience that wouldn't happen again. There, the time had seemed almost magical, aided and abetted by the anonymity of it all. Here, back in her home town, nearly in the arms of a man who was renowned for international conquest, she could maintain control.

That was why, just this once, she was willing to allow the kiss that was feathering against her lips. A kiss was certainly not a lifetime commitment. What harm could it do?

She lifted her arms to put them around his neck, leaning into the soft embrace. Dave wasn't going to be as difficult to handle as she'd first thought. While his hand moved lightly to her back, moving up and down her bare skin, there was nothing threatening or demanding in his touch. In fact, she thought as her mobile lips moved under his, he seemed perfectly content with the almost-tentative kiss. As if he had no intention of taking any thing she wasn't willing to offer. He was so nice, she thought as her fingers curled in the crisp hair brushing his collar. She had been horribly nervous coming here with him this evening. Only her desire not to appear like a skittery schoolgirl had kept her from backing out. She'd been afraid, when put to the test of rejecting his incredible male stamina, that she'd fail.

But Dave was turning out to be quite harmless. That steely male strength she'd seen in the locker room must have been exaggerated by the sheer shock of having him show up out of the blue. This was the gentle, easygoing man who'd taken her riding on the carrousel. Who'd kissed her as they rode in the caboose of the little red train. And who'd laughed about his inability to know a thing about car engines. Something that many men would never admit, feeling it diminished their machismo, somehow. This Dave Barrie she could handle. All she'd have to do was move away or make a single word of protest. She was safe, after all.

The knowledge warmed her, making her willing to experiment. As those long fingers danced an erotic rhythm along her spine, her hand moved on his chest, rubbing in sensuous circles against the crisp shirt. Jan felt the short intake of breath; but his lips, as they left hers to scatter little kisses along her jaw, didn't become more demanding. They were as light as newly fallen snowflakes. It was nice, Jan decided. But she needed more. Just a little bit more.

Lulled by the security in his laconic caresses, Jan pressed her lips lightly against the base of Dave's throat, where he'd opened the top button of his shirt after discarding the slim tie. She could feel the beat of his pulse increase under her kiss and tentatively tasted of the warm skin with the tip of her tongue. She could feel as well as hear the muffled groan rumbling in his throat, but his light caresses didn't change.

Dave Barrie, Jan was discovering, possessed self-discipline himself. It didn't surprise her to learn that she hadn't cornered the market, but the knowledge did create something of a challenge. She had to wonder just what it would take to make him crumble. Just a bit. Her fingers moved to unbutton the shirt, her lips sampling each bit of freed skin. A surreptitious glance upward showed that his eyes were shut to the prolonged torture, bronze curly lashes resting on his cheeks. But still the hands, which were massaging at the base of her spine, didn't clench her skin. Nor did they tremble with physical need.

When she'd unbuttoned the last button, Jan slid her hands around to his back, under the crisp dress shirt. As her fingers explored his muscled back, she pulled him toward her, pressing his warm chest against her breasts. His groan was harsher now, coming from somewhere deep in his chest, and Jan heard herself answering with a soft feminine sound. She welcomed the return of his mouth to hers, his lips plucking at her skin as if to mold them to a shape he preferred. Her softly parted lips opened, the tip of her tongue darting out to trace the firm outline of his teasing lips.

"Oh, my God, Jan," he growled, his hands lowering to her hips, where they moved to draw her into a more intimate embrace. She could feel the stirring of male desire against her and the very idea that she was responsible for it stirred something deep within her. Something that sent a tingling warmth spreading itself outward to reach the very tips of her fingers. She helped him fit her slender frame to the hard lines of his body, sliding downward onto the firm surface of the alabaster white couch, pulling him to cover her.

His hands began making heated paths up and down her body, which arched against him in erotic remembrance, begging for his continued touch. Her renowned self-control, Jan was discovering belatedly, was disappearing like dry autumn leaves in a stiff breeze. Ragged whimpers of sheer need escaped Jan's lips, which opened fully, like a late-summer rosebud, inviting the harsh, thrusting tongue that gained entrance past the barrier of her strong white teeth.

As his hands cupped her small, firm breasts and his long fingers caressed and teased her nipples to hard buds, Jan felt as if shafts of electricity were shooting through her. A spiraling need engulfed her, a need that went beyond anything she'd experienced. Including that night in Phoenix.

His knee moved to part her thighs, their bodies molded together, threatening to cause the material barrier to go up in flames at any moment.

"I want you so much," he rasped against her lips, filling her mouth with harsh, warm breath. "I've been going out of my mind wondering how I'd ever find you again!"

The reference to that shared night, which she'd hoped to never have to face again, should have made Jan's desire wane. But as Dave's body trembled in desperate need, echoing his ragged declaration, she knew that she, too, had been dying inside for this ecstasy. It was as if she were an eagle; having discovered free flight, she'd never be content to remain in the safety of the nest again. Dave Barrie had taught Jan the heights she was capable of soaring to, and now he had returned to her. She shed her last vestige of control, moving against him in a way that left no doubt as to her surrender.

"Please, Dave," she whispered, her hand moving between them to stroke him with intimate need. "Please love me."

"I do, Jan. I thought I'd made that clear," he groaned, his hips surging into the embrace, promising untold delights with the throbbing hardness that was so evident just under his slacks. "Do you love me?"

"I want you, Dave," she cried out softly as his hands slid down the zipper of her waistband. A moment after her body felt it, Jan's mind realized that Dave had frozen, his taut muscles becoming disturbingly still.

"Want?" His blue eyes captured and held her confused gaze by the sheer strength of his will.

There was an underlying tension in the tone, and Jan shivered in response. Her hands moved upward to curl in the soft ginger hair on his chest, moving in enticing little patterns. She smiled uncertainly, a smile that offered him far more than he seemed willing to take at this moment.

"Want?" he asked again on an unmistakably husky note. "I thought we were talking about love."

Jan's green eyes widened, fanned by lush black

lashes as she blinked. Once, then twice again, attempting to collect her scattered senses.

"Making love sounds so much nicer than having sex, Dave." She was returning to earth far faster than she would have preferred. In fact, for a soaring eagle, this was turning out to be one heck of a nose dive.

"I agree. But I don't think we're on quite the same wavelength here, darlin'. I want you. I want to make love to you. But what makes it special, Jan, at least for me, is that I *love* you."

"You can't!" Her eyes moved rapidly over his face, shock and doubt filling the clearing depths.

"Why not?" he asked calmly. "You're not exactly unlovable, you know."

"You don't know me," she argued.

"I know you."

"Men don't fall in love at first sight."

He was very still. Frighteningly so. "How about women?" he challenged.

Jan didn't like the way this conversation was going. She refused to talk about love. He might be able to bandy the word about like it was nothing, but what they'd experienced wasn't love. And Jan wasn't fool enough to get all misty-eyed and think it was.

"Not women with any sense," she said firmly.

"Well, then," he answered, sitting up to rebutton his shirt, "I suppose it's time to eat. That is what I promised you, isn't it? And for a man who's always prided himself on keeping his word, I haven't done very well at feeding you dinner. Other things seem to keep interfering."

He gave her a wicked grin, his expression turning to one of bridled, friendly lust.

"Dave—" Jan's eyes were limpid green pools, inviting him back to the pleasure they'd shared.

"Uh uh, honey. I've got a certain amount of pride. I couldn't live with myself in the morning if I allowed you to think of me as nothing but a sex object at night." The smile was teasing, but his words were strangely serious.

"I promise to respect you in the morning."

Dave tucked in the shirt she'd pulled loose. Dressed once again, he extended a hand to her, pulling her off the couch to stand in the circle of his arms.

"That's nice," he agreed, his look warm and appreciative. "But I've got a fair amount of patience, Jan. I'm willing to wait until you can love me in the morning."

He dropped a quick kiss onto her lips before turning to disappear through a pair of swinging doors. The sounds of pans rattling demonstrated he'd begun dinner, but Jan wasn't quite ready to face him.

She stood gazing down at the moonlit velvety waters, her mind numb with confusion. She knew that she wanted him. Her body, even now, gave proof to that. She knew that the day and night they'd spent together had been the most memorable of her life. Surpassing, incredibly enough, her Olympic experiences at Munich. She also knew she liked him. Who wouldn't? But love?

There was something about Dave Barrie that made her nervous. A strength that went beyond that rock-hard self-confidence. She could feel it. Lurking just under that friendly, easygoing exterior.

How in the world could Jan figure out how she felt about Dave Barrie until she figured out the man himself? Could he actually be so convinced he was in love with her? Had he really meant that startling declaration? And, if so, what must it be like to know your own mind so well?

Jan sighed, abandoning the dilemma for the moment. She took a deep breath, put a cheery smile on her face, and headed toward the kitchen.

Chapter Five

❦

The dinner Dave prepared was a simple, but satisfying meal of grilled steak, tossed green salad, and toasted French bread. Despite their earlier impasse, Jan found herself relaxing and enjoying his good company, enough that when they returned to Coronado she didn't object to a walk along the beach.

"Dave," she asked, breaking the silvery silence that had surrounded them in the night air, "why are you here? In San Diego?"

"To find you?" he asked cheerfully, a hopeful grin on his face as he looked down into hers.

"Truth," she insisted quietly.

"It's no big thing, honey. Just one man's personal, midlife decision."

"Don't you mean crisis?"

Dave considered her words for a long moment. Then he shook his head. "No, it's not as bad as all that. I've just reached a fork in the road and need some time to figure out which path to take."

So the man was human after all. Even Dave Barrie was subject to some doubts. Jan realized his decision was more personal than professional.

"If you don't want to discuss it—"

"Jan, there's nothing you and I can't discuss. Remember that." His blue eyes were almost stern as he watched her, seemingly satisfied when her head dipped in a slight nod. He sank down onto the sand, which still held some warmth from the day's sun, inviting her to join him. His arm comfortably about her shoulders, he stared out across the silvery path gleaming on the black sea.

"First of all, I'm in San Diego because I love the city. I joined the navy here, ended my tour of duty here, and stayed to go to college. After graduation, I got a job working at KNET and was there nine months when the network offered me a chance. From then on, it was a piece of cake. I was in the right place at the right time with the looks and skills they wanted. And, most important, I was willing to go anywhere and everywhere they needed a correspondent. In staff conferences, I was always the guy jumping up, volunteering to go. I've lived that way for the past twelve years."

"You must have seen a lot."

His cheek brushed the top of her head, his breath warm as it fanned her hair. "I have. More than most, I suppose. But I've grown a little weary of it all. I'm here seeking a new goal. A cable outfit has offered me a weekly news program doing an in-depth analysis of the top story of the week. I think I'd like that."

"What about the network?"

"I don't think the network brass is taking me very seriously. Some of them attribute my recent change of heart to overwork. Others seem to think I'm just playing games because my contract's up for renewal. I've got three months left on it and enough accumulated vacation time to spend it all just loafing while I make up my mind. If I wanted to."

Jan was beginning to understand this man and ventured a guess. "But you'd go crazy with three months off."

Dave grinned, that beautiful, devastating grin that created a golden glow to warm her in response. "You've got it, babe. So we compromised. I use the three months working here for the affiliate, feeding some stories to the network. Then I come up with a final decision."

"Which will be . . . ?"

Jan felt the shoulders lift behind her back in a careless shrug. "I haven't the faintest idea."

"I watched you tonight," she offered softly, her hand on his bent knee, unconsciously rubbing the material.

His hand covered hers, twisting so their fingers were entwined. "I'm glad." He paused, then, almost self-consciously, asked, "What did you think?"

"Are you by any chance digging for a compliment?" She smiled, returning the light pressure of his fingers against hers.

"I think I am . . . but only if it's sincere. . . . You don't have to be afraid of hurting my feelings. I'm tough."

Jan hadn't any doubts about that. She'd seen signs of that inner strength. But she had no problem. "I think you looked wonderful. And you've got a marvelous voice for television. But I'm afraid I wasn't paying a lot of attention to what you were saying," she admitted on a crooked grin, recalling the seductive words her evocative memory had conjured up.

"Then we're even there, darlin'. Because I watched that tape of you at least ten times. And not once could I concentrate on the interview. That suit, by the way, should be illegal."

"That suit happens to be my working outfit, Dave Barrie. It's not that different from your sincere blue pinstripes."

"Ah, but my suit could never get me arrested.

Which yours, if you were ever to wear it on the street, could. It's a good thing I'm not a jealous man."

Jan chose to ignore the possessive tone lacing through his deep voice, totally at odds with his light assertion. He'd already informed her that he'd staked his claim, and as blatantly chauvinistic as that statement had been, Jan had the eerie feeling that he meant it. Then again, intent was one thing; reality quite another.

"I did absorb enough to know that you're doing a series on drugs in sports," she changed the subject back to his work. She'd had the thought buzzing around in her head like a pesky insect and knew if she didn't get an answer it would continue to disturb her. "Is that why you came to see me?"

"You've got to be kidding." His expression appeared sincerely incredulous.

"No. It would make sense. I'm certainly a visible person in the city's sports field. And if you're as good as I've been told, you wouldn't turn down a chance for some juicy quotes."

He didn't answer immediately, taking his time to make a long, studied appraisal of her face. The laughter had disappeared from the blue eyes, and they were now unreadable.

"Do you happen to have any of these juicy quotes available? Any scandals of locker-room drug deals, anything like that?"

"Of course not!"

"Then I'd suggest you forget about it. I'll readily admit to wanting something from you, Jan. But an inside track to a story sure isn't it."

She didn't offer a sign of protest as his hand encircled the back of her neck, drawing her to him for a kiss. His mouth brushed against hers, his tongue tenderly tracing the bottom lip where her teeth had bitten through the tender skin earlier in the evening. An involuntary sigh escaped her lips as the mastery of his mouth moving against them recreated that heady, rosy cloud swirling about her head.

Dave's kiss deepened, the tip of his tongue insinuating itself into her mouth, flicking like a finger of flame against the sensitive skin of her cheek. It circled between her lips and teeth, the little forays introducing a delirium that threatened to overwhelm her. Jan leaned into the embrace, her tingling body feeling deprived as he ended it all too soon.

As they walked slowly back down the deserted beach, it seemed as if all Jan's senses were conspiring to amplify the dizzy, dancing way she felt. A falling star blazed through the purple velvet of the sky, its final brilliant flare corresponding with the fire flaming through her veins. Moon dust was sprinkled in his hair, turning the tawny ginger to a liquid copper, and her fingers itched to reach up and play with the curls that just brushed the top of his collar. The sighing of the waves as the sea kissed the shore echoed her own soft sighs of contentment. Jan clung to the warmth of his hand, breathing in the scent of oleanders and a heady, uniquely masculine scent that swirled in her head like incense.

"Tomorrow night?" They were finally standing in front of her door, the porch light casting long, amber shadows around them.

"I can't," Jan answered with honest regret. "I'll be in Long Beach. We've got a meet." Why did that little down quirk of his lips bother her so? "But I'll be back the day after tomorrow," she added.

"What time?"

Jan knew now why she'd added that last part. In order to see that brilliant, happy smile once again. Its wattage was incredible. If they could find a way to harness it, they could light all of San Diego County.

"Probably around six. Or seven. I'm driving."

"I'll be here, waiting on your front porch like a lost puppy."

Jan had the impression the man had never felt lost a day in his life, but it was an appealing image. She'd see him just one more time. Because he made her feel so good. Then she'd call a halt to this entire relationship before she got in too deeply. She was a grown woman. Used to handling men. What could one more evening hurt?

He bent down to kiss her on the lips with far too circumspect a kiss. Then, touching his palm to her cheek, he said softly, "Sweet dreams, darlin'," and turned, heading down the sidewalk to his car.

Jan watched the amber taillights of the BMW disappear down the road, trying to keep them in view as they merged with the other traffic heading toward the magnificent span bridging Coronado with the mainland. Finally, she gave up her attempt, closing the door and leaning against it, her head spinning with a variety of conflicting sensations.

Jan felt like Rip Van Winkle. Dave Barrie had awakened her to so many new feelings. It was almost as if she'd been asleep all these years, waiting for him to introduce her to the world. She'd never laughed as much as she had that blissful day in Phoenix. She knew she'd never felt as carefree as she did with him. And she had to admit that she'd never felt so desirable. Or felt such an attraction for a man. But love? Jan shook her head as she prepared for bed.

There was still a very strong part of her urging caution, telling her to hold back. Dave Barrie may appear to be the scarlet thread who was lacing himself through the dull fabric of her life, but he was a stranger. A wonderful, passionate stranger. And despite the enticing camouflage of that smiling, easygoing man, she still sensed he was dangerous. To the core.

Remembering his words, Jan found herself constantly applying cream to her sun-exposed lips the following day. But she was a lip-biter when under stress, and the importance of this competition gave the sun block a life expectancy of three to five minutes before it had been eaten off. She wondered, idly, what the caloric content of Chapstick was.

Jan was a professional, and the image of Dave's constantly cheerful face with its ready smile and dancing blue eyes didn't interfere with her coaching. It was just between events that Dave seemed to be there beside her, warming her with his presence to a heat that had nothing to do with the bright yellow sun overhead.

That night, however, in the motel room, was when the memory of him made her ache with longing. The room was like every other motel room in the world—hard bed, flat pillows, television bolted to the dresser, and the inevitable seascape on the wall. It was the same as any Jan had ever been in. And it was the same as Dave Barrie's room in Phoenix. Her head was filled with him, like an inhaled drug, infiltrating all the cavities of her mind. His virile scent lingered in her memory, and her body warmed at the recollection of his lovemaking.

Jan rolled over onto her stomach, pulling the pillow tightly over her head, as if she could shut out the caressing words she was hearing, the voice in her mind soft and alluring. But they continued to flow over her, refusing to give her peace.

She was awake, agonizing over Dave, when she heard the surreptitious closing of a door across the motel courtyard. Moving to the window, Jan drew aside the draperies slightly to watch young Jimmy Cassidy as he crept through the night shadows, headed in the direction of the Redlands' club. She'd been hearing whispered rumors all day. A party. A compassionate, wry smile formed on her lips. She could stop him right now, but it would be a far better lesson for him to learn on his own.

She sighed heavily, thinking, not for the first time, that she wouldn't want to be sixteen again for anything in the world. Returning to the rumpled, lonely bed, where she continued to toss and turn, Jan wondered if there was an ideal age. An age when life was simple and easy and you didn't have to feel like a salmon, constantly battling your way upstream.

Jan watched the scores being held up by the three judges. Jimmy Cassidy was definitely showing the results of a bad night. He hadn't scored well on the six required dives. There was still the outside chance, of course, that his four voluntary dives could bring him up in the standings. However, due to his inexperience at this level of dual competition, Jan had chosen to keep the level of difficulty fairly low on the dives, opting instead for proficiency. Something that he seemed to have left behind in the Redlands' motel room last night.

While his hips had been properly flexed in the pike position, Jan wanted to scream as his right knee bent. Just a hair, but enough to catch the eagle-eyed scrutiny of the judges. It should have been a good dive. A forward, one and a half somersault, pike position, from the tower. But he hadn't pulled in tightly enough, going over from the perfect ninety-degree entry as he splashed into the water.

"I heard the kid was dynamite. Looks like his fuse got a little damp."

Jan turned from her scowling perusal of the scores to view the owner of the all-too-familiar, mocking voice.

"Hello, Jon," she greeted her former coach and husband. "He *is* good." Her back stiffened a little in defense, like a mother bear protecting a cub. "He just spent last night celebrating a bit prematurely."

Jon's teak face had a smug, knowing expression. "The Redlands' party."

Jan nodded. "The same. Rough way to learn a lesson, but I don't think I'll have any more problems with him. This is going to be about as much humiliation as he's going to want to subject himself to for a very long time."

Dark-brown eyes observed her with undisguised censure. "You're not hard enough on them, Jan. You should keep a closer eye on those kids so this stuff doesn't happen."

She lifted her bronze shoulders in a careless shrug. She'd grown used to this. The procedure was always the same. Jon had controlled her every waking moment when she'd been his wife. And his championship diver. Now, whenever they met, he seemed determined to train her on how to coach.

"We have different methods, Jon," she replied quietly. "We can't all be Vince Lombardi. I like to think my job is to coax their diving, not run their lives."

"As you say," he replied smoothly, returning his attention to the women's platform event that was beginning, "we have different ideas."

Despite the poor showing from the newest member of the team, La Conquista did well, placing second in the Southern California meet. Since the team was young, Jan felt they had a good chance to put a diver into one of the four slots on the Olympic team.

Driving back in her roomy car filled with teenagers, Jan noted that Jimmy had zonked out, his head against the side of the window as he slept, oblivious to the constant loud chatter around him. His slightly pewter-gray complexion and the green-around-the-gills attitude gave credence to the rumor that the bathtub of the motel room had been filled with ice. And spiked watermelon. Slabs and slabs of it.

She gave him a glance in the rearview mirror. Poor kid. It must've hurt like hell, hitting the water from that height with a stomachache like he undoubtedly had. But she wouldn't have to worry about him again. He was in the big time now, and she had no doubt he'd behave like it. Used to taking every medal in smaller meets, he'd been disconsolate not to even finish in the top ten.

Jan sighed lightly, the sound hidden by the raucous noise of the Led Zeppelin rock tape one of the kids had stuck in her tape player.

The forest-green European sedan was pulling up to her house as Jan arrived home.

"We've got perfect timing," Dave said. He dropped a light kiss on her lips, took her suitcase from her hand, and headed up the steps to her front door. "Have you noticed how you always seem to be driving into my life at precisely the right moment?"

"I would suppose, then," Jan replied, turning the key in the lock and opening the door, "that it's *I* who has the perfect timing."

"Ah—but I always manage to be in just the right spot at the right time. It's kismet, fate, and collaboration, darlin'. We do everything well together." He bestowed a warm, intimate smile upon her.

Jan gestured for him to leave the suitcase inside the front door as she made her way to the kitchen.

"Well, I sure hope we cook well together, because I'm too beat to go out."

"Hmm. Not exactly the kitchen of Julia Child."

Dave was standing before the open, almost-empty cupboard, staring at the half-loaf of white bread, two boxes of instant chocolate pudding, a bottle of olive oil, six saltine crackers, and a jar of beef bouillon cubes.

"You've found me out. When we're preparing for a meet, I forget everything. I've been told I have an obsessive personality." Jan looked over her shoulder with jade eyes that handed him a warning.

"Great. Then when you finally realize you're in love with me, I'll have it made. I can't imagine anything I'd rather be than one of your obsessive habits."

"The only habit you should be thinking about right now is eating," she snapped, far too tired to joke about that subject. It had occurred to her, in the gray and pink shadows of dawn, that she'd never felt about anyone the way she was feeling about Dave. It had teased and tickled about her mind, tantalizing her, hinting at the word "love." But she'd consistently pushed the idea back down. Love didn't happen this soon. And even if it did, she wouldn't feel so uneasy about it, would she? Love was supposed to make you feel happy all the time. Giddy. Like your blood was infused with sparkling water.

"We can always have toast," Dave offered helpfully, eyeing the bread.

Jan untwisted the wire tie to peer into the plastic bag. "Not unless you've developed a taste for penicillin."

"A little green?"

"Let me put it this way," she answered, tossing the moldy bread into the trash, "if you happen to have strep throat, I'd suggest the toast. If you're healthy and wish to remain that way, I'd recommend the bouillon and crackers."

She slumped down onto a bar stool, swiveling it back and forth as she eyed the cupboard bleakly. "I don't think we're going to have any better luck in the refrigerator," she announced. "I'm sorry, Dave."

"No problem. We'll go to a place where the kitchen is always open."

"Maybe some other time. I'm really exhausted." From tossing and turning over you all night, she could have added, deciding that in this case, silence was definitely golden.

"You'll be able to lie down and take your shoes off," he coaxed.

"Your place." Her green eyes were solemn. "It's not going to be that easy, Dave. I've already decided that if you want this relationship to continue, we've got to start over."

He folded his arms across his chest, observing her from his superior height. "Starting over is not exactly continuing," he pointed out. "And I happen to think we're going along just fine the way we are. Granted, things will improve when you're willing to admit how you feel. We both might start getting a decent night's rest. But other than that, I wouldn't change a thing."

"This relationship isn't real," she argued, rubbing her fingers wearily on her temples. God, she wished she hadn't brought it up. She was so tired! "It didn't start out right, and just because I behaved that way in Phoenix doesn't mean you can expect it as a matter of course."

"I don't," he said simply. "I'm willing to let it drop for tonight, Jan. I can tell you're dead on your feet. But this foolishness that I only represent a crazed moment better off forgotten is taking off on the wrong track, honey." He took her hand from

where it was rubbing restless circles on her forehead and placed it between his palms, scattering a
sprinkling of light kisses on the inside of her wrist.

"Face it, Jan, sweetheart," he closed the conversation brightly, "your chickens have come home to
roost. And this is one motivated rooster you've got
here."

Jan leaned back in the bucket seat of Dave's car,
opening her eyes when she could feel him slowing
for the approach to the Coronado Bridge. She
enjoyed, as she always did, the wide sweep of the
expanse, its graceful, curving arch lit by amber
lights.

"I love the bridge," he murmured. "They did a
beautiful job. But I miss the ferries."

She turned her head on the leather upholstery,
looking at him in surprise. "You do? You know, I
realize the bridge makes commuting to the mainland much easier, but there was something so
thrilling about driving your car into the caverns of
those big, creaky old boats. When I was little, I used
to pretend I was crossing the high seas on a pirate
ship. I was always the stowaway. Who, of course,
became the cabin boy and discovered the buried
treasure."

"A stowaway, perhaps," he commented, sliding a
glance in her direction as they crossed the delicate-
appearing span. "But a boy? Never. You grew up
here?"

Jan nodded. "In the house I'm living in now,
actually. My parents wanted a freer life-style and
bought a condominium in Rancho Bernardo. I was
divorced, looking for a place to live, so I bought the
house from them. It seemed like the best deal for all
of us."

"How long ago?" His voice was casual.

"Ages." Jan thought for a moment. "More than

ten years now. Funny how time just disappears behind you." And pain, too, she considered. Jon hadn't even been able to hurt her today. Or make her feel she needed his approval.

"Funny," Dave agreed, looking thoughtful as he kept his attention directed to the road for the rest of the trip.

"Can I get you something? A glass of wine?" Dave flicked the silent switch as they entered, bathing them in that gold-and-silver glow.

"Wine would be nice," Jan agreed. She watched as he moved to the silver-backed bar. "Dave?"

"Yeah, honey?"

Honey. It came so easily off his lips. He probably said it as a reflex habit after traveling all these years. It would be easier than keeping names straight. Jan sighed, twisting a lock of hair around her finger. Why did she even care?

"Did you mean it when you said I could take my shoes off?"

"Of course. Take off anything you like. In fact, do you need help with anything? Buttons? Zippers? Hooks?"

"My shoes will be sufficient."

He grinned wolfishly. "Spoilsport."

Jan slipped off the flat sandals, wiggling her toes in the plush white rug under her feet. Dave poured the golden California chablis and joined her, handing her a glass. He sat farther down the sofa from her than she was expecting. Jan was attempting to decide why that disappointed her when he put his wineglass down on the chrome-and-glass table in front of them and, reaching down, grabbed her ankles. With a single deft motion, he swung her legs up onto the couch, her feet in his hands as he began to massage them gently, fingers working along her arches.

"Didn't your mother ever tell you not to put your feet up on your furniture?" she murmured, enjoying the smooth, firm ministrations of his hands.

"Hush. It's not my furniture. It's the network's. Remember?"

His hands bent her toes, rubbed the soles of her feet, concentrating on the arches; then his thumbs began making smooth little circles at her ankles. Jan had been worked on by a variety of athletic trainers, but none had ever possessed the sweet touch of Dave Barrie. His palms worked up to her calves, kneading the muscles at the back.

"Tense. Hard as a rock. I think you need the works, babe."

Jan moved her gaze from the hands on her legs to his bright blue eyes. "The works?"

"You're as tight as the mainspring on an overwound alarm clock, darlin'," he answered. "I'd say the last two days were rougher on you than you'd care to admit."

And the night. Don't forget the night. The solitary darkness filled with the husky deep voice of this man, his touch, his scent. Everything about him had mushroomed in her mind, filling every pocket with his presence.

"That's your diagnosis," she said. "What's your prescription?" Nothing like giving a man a slow, inside curve with the bases loaded, Jan considered. She was just asking for trouble with that question. Trouble she'd have to admit she wanted.

"A warm bath and a home-cooked meal. We'll have you back to a new woman in no time."

"Don't you like the woman you've got?" It was a soft, enticing purr that was unmistakably inviting.

Dave's eyes glittered like many-faceted sapphires. "I'm wild about the woman I've got," he answered on a gravelly, vibrating tone. "So wild, in fact, that I'm doing my damnedest to put her welfare before my admittedly selfish desires."

He swung her feet back onto the floor. "There's a tub through that door you won't believe, Jan. Indulge yourself while I start dinner."

Dave unfolded his long length from the rigid sofa, giving her an affectionate look. A flare of unmasked desire rose in the blue eyes, and he sighed lightly before heading through the swinging doors to the kitchen.

Jan was exhausted and had to admit a few minutes in a warm bath sounded enticing. She rose wearily, heading off in the direction he'd indicated.

The man was definitely not making exaggerated promises about the bath. Jan gasped as she entered the room. Again, all the walls were mirrored and delineated with chrome vertical strips at two-foot intervals. The entire room was a mirror, including the ceiling. Jan looked up, seeing the bathtub reflected above her head. Bathtub? She'd seen swimming pools that weren't much bigger. A person could probably swim laps in the thing, if they were inclined. Of course, she considered, anyone with a setup like this probably indulged in quite a different type of exercise altogether!

The floor was covered with a silky plush carpet the color of milkweed that continued up the three steps onto the raised platform of the sunken tub. The black marble was veined with gold, a color echoed by the gleaming fixtures. Rows of crystal jars filled with red and yellow and green salts and oils were neatly arranged on glass shelves over the jet-black marble sinks. Lifting the lids and sniffing until she found one that had an oriental scent, Jan turned on the water, pouring a liberal amount of the jade crystals into the swirling depths.

The tiny beads immediately turned the water into a deep herbal green, sending whispers of san-

dalwood, jasmine, amber, and musk into a heady
cloud that swirled upward. Feeling like the newest
addition to a sultan's harem, Jan took off her clothing and placed it in a neat pile on an ivory velvet
chair. Then she lowered herself into the steaming
waters, sighing with the sheer, luxurious pleasure
of it all.

Resting her head back against the wide gold rim,
Jan saw a switch and flipped it up to see what
would happen. She jumped as the water began
churning in all directions around her, bubbling
between her legs, slapping green waves against her
breasts, creating frothy breakers on the surface. A
spa. Damned if there wasn't a built-in Jacuzzi in
this thing. The bubbling, churning waters mas-
saged her body, turning her to the consistency of
wet spaghetti.

Much, much later, realizing it was only a matter
of moments before she'd be perfectly content to just
allow herself to drift below the surface, Jan turned
off the switch and pulled herself reluctantly from
the velvet cling of the water. The dense, rich per-
fume surrounded her in its sensuous mist, com-
bining with the weakness in her limbs to make her
dizzy, and she grasped hold of the chrome rail
embedded in the glass wall.

"Sea legs, that's what you've got." She giggled to
herself, feeling her legs wobbling beneath her like
so much warm Jell-O as she reached for the stack of
plush, buttermilk-white towels. "Need to get your
land legs back, Jan old girl."

Wrapping the soft terry bath sheet around herself, Jan stumbled out of the fragrant steam of the
bathroom into the adjoining bedroom.

"I'll just take a little rest before dinner," she
decided, pitching drunkenly on her watery legs
toward the vast bed. She deliberately fell forward,

face-first, onto the cool satin of the black comforter, landing with a soft plop on the mattress.

"A water bed! I just did a belly flop onto a water bed," she murmured, giggling whimsically to herself. God, she was tired. The glass of wine, encouraged by the warm bath, seemed to have sped directly to her head. She closed her eyes and concentrated on the waves she'd created with her nose dive.

Chapter Six

"Now that's what I like—an obedient woman."

The deep, resonant bass tones brought Jan's green eyes open. Turning her head, she stared into a pair of well-shaped, denim-clad thighs.

"Come down here," she ordered groggily. "It's too damn difficult to carry on a conversation with a leg."

"Obedient and inviting. Gets better and better." There was amused affection in the voice originating from somewhere high above the hard blue thigh.

Jan felt the motion of the mattress underneath her body as Dave joined her, sitting on the edge of the bed. Struggling, she managed to prop her head up with a palm, her elbow resting precariously on the undulating mattress.

"What do you mean, obedient?"

"I tell the lady to go relax and that's exactly what she does. I don't think you could look any looser if you'd been poured onto that bed through a sieve, sweetheart."

Jan rolled over onto her back, stretching her arms above her head like a lazy, luxuriously pampered cat. "I don't think I've ever felt so wonderful," she murmured. "Wait a minute. One other time—"

The siren in her brain shut off her mouth seconds

before revealing the intimate knowledge that the only other time she'd felt this good was when she awoke after spending the night with him. A red flush appeared on her chest above the white bath sheet.

"Interesting. Do you always blush on your chest like that?"

Dave touched his fingertips along the slight rise of her breasts above the towel, leaving a little white trail as his finger indented the skin.

"Temperature two hundred degrees Fahrenheit," he determined.

The color rose to her face.

"Hmmm." The treacherous fingertips traced along her collarbone, then ran enticingly up to her hot, crimson cheekbones. "Three hundred degrees and rising," he murmured. His fingers were making lazy little circles on her heated skin. "Three hundred and fifty. Four hundred. Five hundred degrees Fahrenheit. I think we've got a slight problem here."

Jan could feel the red flames shooting up her scalp under her damp hair. Dave put one hand on the far side of her, leaning over to brush her hair away from her scarlet forehead with his free hand. His own face was a scant few inches from her, and the crystal-blue eyes held all the intensity of a physical caress.

"Hmmm," he continued, his head lowering, "we seem to be endangering our heat shield, Mission Control. What would you suggest our next maneuver be?"

Jan could feel the warm feathering of his breath against her lips, which were tingling with anticipation. Her luminous eyes gleamed with moisture, brightening the emerald sheen.

"A kiss would be nice."

There was a husky catch to his voice. "Oh, darlin', I thought you'd never ask."

His lips lowered to whisper over her mouth, the light touch sweet and unthreatening. They brushed against the corners of her mouth, creating a teasing, tantalizing need. Jan parted her tingling lips on a supplicant sigh, and the passion that had been hidden so close to the surface sprang to life. Dave drank from her mouth like a parched man coming across a cool, sparkling oasis in the burning desert. Their tongues sought each other's out, twisting and meeting in remembered ecstasy, desire escalating like a pilot light turned to full heat, burning with a dancing, rising flame.

"Please, Dave . . . oh, yes . . . please . . ." Her lips, her hoarse whispers, the beseeching look in Jan's misty green eyes, all requested and received the domination he brought to the kiss.

"I love you, Jan . . . I really do . . ." Dave kissed her chin, her cheeks, the tip of her nose, her eyes. He tasted her face, the tantalizing lips never ceasing as his hands moved to unfold the thick towel. "Oh, babe . . . I do so love you!"

Jan turned fully in his arms, the white terry falling away as he pulled her on top of him. Jan gasped as he took one breast in his mouth, his tongue and teeth coming into play to leave a wet, stinging warmth. As he abandoned the responsive breast, to treat the other to the same savage assault, Dave gave a deep growl of surrender, sounding like a wounded animal.

Jan moved against him, feeling the stirring hardness underneath her as Dave became lost in his fierce male need. She didn't want to dissect these feelings, she didn't want to worry about their source. All she cared for at the moment was the glorious sensations he was creating, his hands burning trails over her hips and thighs, his lips sending shafts of pure passion through her in a white-hot flame.

Dave's heart was pounding, Jan could feel it as he dragged his mouth back to recapture her lips, pressing her to the hard, aroused length of him. The wild throbbing was beating against her bared breasts, and his breathing was shallow and harsh as he rasped warmth into the moist darkness of her mouth.

Jan whimpered her spiraling urgency, writhing against him with impatience as his hands grabbed her flesh. He pulled her against him in a brutal, but at the same time blissful embrace. Her desperate moans were unintelligible, but she was communicating her desire to him in more primitive fashion, her hips moving against his in feminine need.

Suddenly, with a harsh, strangled cry, Dave was no longer under her, but standing beside the bed, his hands visibly shaking as they thrust through his tawny mussed hair.

"I won't . . ." he gasped on a choked, horrible sound. "I just can't do it. Not like this."

Jan's head was spinning and something was withering inside her. Like a leaf dying and turning black and cold. Her fingers curled into her palm, her hand pressed against her lips to stop the sobs that were threatening to break loose.

What was the matter with him? She knew he wanted her. The evidence of that was still solidly visible as he paced back and forth. Finally, he strode over to the glass wall, a replica of the one in the living room, and gazed out over the jet-black waters of the bay. His hands were thrust deep into the front pockets of his jeans and Jan watched his shoulders rise and fall as he drank in ragged gulps of breath.

"Dave," she whispered, trying out her voice and

finding it to be weak and thin, "you weren't taking anything I wasn't offering."

She stared at the broad back, wondering if he'd even heard her. Not knowing what else to say, Jan fell silent, waiting.

When Dave finally turned around, his blue eyes were as bleak as a tomb. "I know. And I'm probably the worst fool that was ever born. But it's not enough, dammit!"

His voice was only barely under control, and Jan watched as his hands curled into tight fists in his pockets. Then he closed those alien eyes and rubbed his chin wearily, his shoulders dropping.

He returned to sit beside her, a far-from-steady hand stroking the back of her head, the fingers curving around her neck to hold her to the intense gaze.

"Jan, I want you so much I can't see straight. I ache from needing you. And I won't shock you with some of the thoughts I've had while lying alone night after night in this damn sex palace." His dark gaze circled the room, encompassing the blatant eroticism of the bedroom and adjoining bath. "But I want all of you. Not just your body. And I know I'll hurt far more if I settle for that. I never settle for second best, babe. It's not my style."

He drew her to him, his mouth covering hers in a long, trembling kiss. She could feel the shudder of his body and felt like weeping.

"I love you, Jan," he repeated as he released her lips. "And right now, if you won't think me a lousy host, I'm going to take a short, solitary walk before we test my willpower any further. Because another two minutes and I'll say the hell with it and do what we both want. And need."

Dave looked at her with so much feeling that Jan thought her heart might stop beating. As far gone as she was, she could detect the edge of desperation in his deep voice. He rose, the motion causing more waves to rock the bed, and he heaved a huge sigh, shaking his head in mute frustration.

"That's really quite provocative, you know, babe," he observed. "I've had some rough assignments in my time, but walking away from you on that overgrown water bottle is proving to be the toughest." The glimmer in those blue eyes needed no translation.

Jan willed the waves to stop, wondering as her body rose and fell in a fluid motion just what kind of network would buy a water bed in the first place. Obviously one that had been watching too many hours of its own programming.

"I'll be back in ten minutes, honey." He managed a crooked grin that didn't quite reach his eyes. "Then we'll eat."

Jan was tossing a green salad when Dave entered the dining room and looked up to be greeted with that vivid, heart-stopping smile. Obviously the walk had done him a world of good.

"You look terrific!"

Jan glanced down at the simple white jeans and the red-and-white-striped top. Terrific? Hardly. Not bad. Even pretty good. But *this* was not terrific.

"I think you're a liar, Dave Barrie."

"I never lie. You look fresh as a daisy. No," he observed, the keen gaze moving from the top of her head down her slender frame and back up again. "Not a daisy," he decided. "A candy cane. You remind a fella of Christmas. Huge snowflakes like Grandma's crocheted doilies. Oranges stuffed with cloves. Macy's. Santa Claus. And—"

"And that's enough." Jan laughed.

How did the man do it? In those few short minutes he'd managed to slide on that affable personality so well that no one would have ever guessed the intense scene in the bedroom had ever occurred. These glimpses of that other Dave Barrie made her uneasy. Was it possible that the uncompromising, dangerous man was the genuine article? And this one nothing but a charming decoy? If so—why? Well, whatever the answer, Jan was too relieved to find herself back in the company of the lovable Dave Barrie and pushed the question aside for the moment.

"You said dinner in ten minutes," she reminded him. "And I don't know about you, but I'm suddenly starving."

"But I promised to cook it for you."

"I'm not a total loss in the kitchen, Dave. Besides, your larder was well-stocked."

"Comes with the territory, darlin'." He grinned. "I wonder if cable television feeds you quite so well."

He pulled out a chair for her, leaning down to nuzzle the back of her neck as he pushed her toward the glass table.

"Gorgeous. The woman even smells like a Christmas garden."

"There aren't Christmas gardens," she argued, placing the linen napkin on her lap, wondering at the decorator's choice of black.

"Poetic license. Besides, there are always Christmas gardens in California." He grated fresh pungent Parmesan cheese over the fettucini Alfredo she'd placed on the table.

"I may not know where I'm going in life," he said, "but I sure know I'm not objecting to where I am right now." He held out the wicker basket of toasted Italian herb bread, offering her a slice. "I think I'll just live out my days smelling the flowers at the back of my beautiful woman's neck."

Her instinctive protective device sounded with the alacrity of a civil-defense siren at his use of the possessive pronoun. She was not *his* woman. She

was not *anyone's* woman but her own. Jan's independence had been hard to come by, a long, painful
process, and she wasn't about to toss it away simply because this man had tapped a well of unfamiliar emotions deep within her. What Dave Barrie
offered was an illusive, fleeting pleasure. If she
could summon up the strength to blink twice, it
would probably all be gone.

Jan realized that the perceptive blue eyes had not
missed her internal conflicts, and she quickly
dropped her distressed gaze to her plate, returning
her full attention to her meal.

"While I was walking along the beach, I decided
on the perfect belated birthday present for you."

She lifted her face to his sparkling eyes. "What?"

"A videotape recorder. Then you can set it to
record the news and watch it when you get home."
He grinned at her with obvious satisfaction, picking
up his fork to spear a shiny spinach leaf.

"Why should I do that? I read the paper. I'm not
illiterate, Dave Barrie."

"I'd like to know you were watching me," he said
simply. "Especially if I take that cable offer."

Jan suddenly had an unbidden image of a harem
of olive-skinned women wrapped in silken veils, sitting around a nineteen-inch color portable, viewing
Dave Barrie as he did his network news thing. She
wondered how many sets and video recorders he'd
purchased for women over the years.

"What's the matter?"

Damn him. He never missed a beat of her heart,
and he certainly hadn't missed the fleeting expression of pain that had just darkened her features.

"Nothing."

"Don't give me that." His voice had an odd, gritty,
threatening quality. "Something just happened.
What was it?"

Jan shook her head. "I was just picturing a tentful of women watching you while the eunuchs were standing guard outside."

Dave's eyes darkened to a deep indigo for a moment, looking like a storm-tossed sea. "For a woman who likes to consider herself well-informed," he replied on a dangerously low note, "I'd say you're reading the wrong paper."

"I didn't read that!" Jan bristled self-defensively. "Maggie told me about it."

"And it's a total fabrication. As was the opera singer in Milan and any other romantic escapade you've read about. I may not have been a monk, but I've always prided myself on discretion. And for your information, Jan Banning Baxter, you're the only woman I've ever given a damn about whether or not she watched me on the air!"

His fist hit the table, causing one golden slice of bread to jump from the wicker basket in response. His tone cracked like a whip, cutting her to the quick.

"Except my mother, when I first began. But I never had to worry about her. She sent me in-depth critiques after every broadcast for the first six months. All rave reviews, of course."

As quickly as the anger had flared, it was gone, and the familiar humor lit his blue eyes again. But Jan realized she'd been handed a warning. There were more layers of complexity to this man than she'd first thought. She kept catching these disturbing, but intriguing glimpses of something that refused to go along with his laid-back, smiling image. The image he put on for, literally, the entire world.

"Let's go into the living room," that familiar, calm voice suggested, "and watch the lights for a while."

He kept laying these sensual little traps and she kept walking right into them. Willingly. If Jan had

an ounce of common sense, she'd reject that suggestion immediately. Any other decision would be fool-
hardy.

"I'd like that," she agreed instead, ignoring
every vestige of reason clamoring to make itself
heard in her brain. "But first let me help you with
the dishes."

"Nope. Take advantage, Jan. I won't always be
living in the lap of such luxury. The housekeeper
will do the dishes. And you're still invited to put
your feet up on the furniture."

He sat in a corner of the sofa, pulling her back so
she was leaning against his chest, her legs stretched
out with his.

"Do you always play with fire like this?" he
asked quietly, his hands clasped over hers, his
thumbs absently brushing her midriff.

"No," she answered softly, honestly. "But then
again, I've never been so tempted before. Or known
anyone capable of inciting such a flame." She
risked a glance upward, her eyes melted emeralds,
and she watched a look of sheer agony twist his
face.

"Oh, Jan," Dave groaned, "I'm doing my best,
babe, but I'm not made of stone." His arms tightened about her, his eyes devouring her uplifted features as if he'd been starving for her far too long.
"Why don't you just admit you love me so we can
stop this ridiculous charade?"

His voice was low and tormented, thick with
grievance, and Jan longed to give in. Just for
tonight. Just so he'd make love to her once again.
Because the one thing she was willing to admit was
just how badly she wanted—needed—him.

"Dave, I can't." A deep-seated trait of honesty
forced the truth. "I can't believe that what we're
experiencing could really be love. Not in this short
a time."

Her palm reached up to brush his cheek, feeling his beard lightly scratching against her skin. How could this man make her feel so wonderful when their situation made her so miserable? All at the same time.

"I hadn't realized there was a timetable for these things. Tell me, Jan—what's the appropriate length of time before you're permitted to fall in love? One week? Two? A month? You'd better let me know the date in advance so I can mark my calendar. I'd hate to be out of town when the scheduled event finally occurs."

Jan knew the sarcasm was only in response to his frustration, but she was still irritated by that damnable self-assurance of his.

"What makes you so certain it will happen at all, Dave? Or is it the usual procedure for women to fall in love with you?"

Her exhaustion was returning, settling about her shoulders like a heavy dark cloud. That, plus the confusion she was experiencing about her feelings for Dave, made Jan pull herself from his arms. She stood with her hands on her hips, glaring down at him.

"You probably have an entire catalog from all your world travels, don't you? The model. The photographer. The actress. I suppose I'll be filed away as the diver, right?"

A muscle jerked along the hard line of Dave's jaw as he swung his feet to the floor, half-rising from the sofa.

"Don't, Jan," he warned softly.

Her only response to the drawled caution was a bitter laugh. "No, with your vast experience," she continued, "you've probably acquired a far more esoteric listing than most. The terrorist. The spy. How about an Interpol agent? Ever have one of them?"

"That's it."

He was on his feet in an instant, long fingers circling her wrist. Before Jan knew it, she was buckled into the front seat of his car, forced into uncomfortable intimacy with the dangerous alter ego of Dave Barrie.

The silence eddied about them on the way home, a living, breathing thing. Finally Jan broke it, her voice tentative.

"When I was a child," she began softly, not receiving any encouragement from the man beside her, "I wanted to dive in the Olympics more than anything in the entire world. I ate, breathed—lived—diving. I would've tried to grow wings, or gills, if I thought it could help. That's all I did for thirteen years. Every single day, all year round."

"That's admirable. For a child to work so hard at something," Dave offered, his attention still on his driving. But, Jan decided, it was a start of a conversation. Encouraged, she carried on.

"I don't know about admirable. It was like breathing—I had no choice."

He turned and nodded, his study of her thoughtful before he returned his attention to the road.

"Then I went to Munich. I did everything I'd been taught and came home with a silver medal."

"You must have been thrilled."

Jan shook her head slowly. "That's what I thought would happen, you know?" She waited, her silence drawing his attention again, her slanted dark-green eyes straining as she sought to make him understand. "But it was devastating. Here I was, at an age when most people are just considering setting a goal, and I'd achieved mine. It was all over."

Jan wasn't surprised, in fact she felt a glimmer of hope, as Dave suddenly pulled the car into a deserted parking lot, killing the engine and turning

in the seat to face her. He pursed his lips thoughtfully, as if running her words through his com-
puterlike mind for an instant replay.

"It must have been hard," he said. "Is that when
your marriage broke up? Were they related?"

"You could say that," she answered in a subdued
voice. "Since I was married to my coach."

"I see."

Suddenly, it was important to get her relationship with Jon and her marriage out in the open. To
dissect it once and for all, then put it away.

"Jon was my life, but diving was my life, too.
They were both intrinsically tied up together. Jon
told me what to eat, when to eat, when to go to bed.
He scheduled every waking minute of my day and
taught me everything I needed to know to win that
medal. I couldn't have done it without him. He was
the best coach in the country. The best coach for
me. I worshiped him."

"Did you love him?" It was a quiet question, but
its importance ricocheted about them in the small
car.

"I thought I did, at the time," Jan answered
truthfully. "But what I loved was his ability. And
he valued me. I was like a lump of modeling clay to
Jon. He could make me into exactly what we both
wanted me to be. It was a little like playing God."

"And an escalator ride to a helluva letdown,"
Dave commented, an unreadable mask on his face.

"It was. All of a sudden my goal was gone. My
husband was ready to find himself another piece of
clay, and I realized I had absolutely no idea what
life was about. I was like one of those people who
wake up after years in a coma. Physically they're all
grown up, but mentally they're infants. I was inca-
pable of taking care of myself. Of making even the
most basic decisions. It was horrible."

"And now that you've learned how to take care of

yourself, you don't want to hand the controls over to anyone else." His tone was quiet, resigned.

Jan nodded solemnly, her eyes pleading for understanding.

Dave turned, flicking the key in the ignition and bringing the car back to life. Its engine purred in the quiet night.

"Well, then, we don't have any problem, Jan. I don't want control of your life. I only want your love. You can keep everything else." He pulled the car back onto the road, his mood still inscrutable.

"Dave?"

"Yes, Jan?"

She felt like screaming at him, like hitting him. Anything to get more reaction than she'd received. Here she'd bared her soul to him, telling him things she'd never revealed to anyone, and he was taking it so damn casually. Well, she'd invited some honesty on his part. If he wasn't going to volunteer, she'd just come out and ask.

"Were you ever married?"

"Yeah. A very long time ago." His voice was flat and didn't encourage further probing.

"What happened?"

"It's a long story, Jan. Not the slightest bit original. I was off on a nine-month cruise. Came home to find out she'd been entertaining more troops than a USO tour. End of story. End of marriage."

"Oh . . . Did you love her?"

"Before or after?"

"Either. Both," she decided.

"Try neither. Where I come from, Jan, there are more basic concerns than those of the heart. Survival, for one. I was fool enough to think she needed me. At the time, she probably did. It was when I wasn't around any longer that she found other guys just as willing to take care of her. And to tell you the truth, it was a relief to let them."

Jan pondered that awhile as the silence encompassed them again.

"Where *are* you from?" she asked, thinking that it must hold the clue to those rough edges she'd witnessed from time to time. Perhaps if she could just understand him . . .

"Not tonight," he said abruptly. "You're too tired to understand, and I'm not in any mood to dwell on it." His tone was firm, and Jan chose not to put it to the test.

She was tired. The quick cure of the bath and the meal had worn off, and the emotional turmoil of this evening had sapped her last vestiges of strength. She was content to lean her head back and close her eyes.

"I want to spend tomorrow with you." They were parked outside her house.

"Can't." Jan mumbled, fatigue evident in her slurred tone. "Gotta work."

"No, I don't. I don't work weekends. Tomorrow's Sunday," he reminded her.

Jan shook her glossy head, which was lolling on her shoulders as if in danger of tumbling off. "Uh uh. Don't understand . . . I work."

His eyes narrowed a little in the spreading glow of the streetlight. "At the club?"

"Uh uh . . . public pool . . . free . . . for underprivileged kids . . ." The disjointed phrases came with deep breaths between them, and her long dark lashes kept resting on her cheeks as she drifted in and out of a light, lazy slumber.

"Fine. I'll come along." Dave opened his door and climbed out, going around the front of the car to open the passenger side. "Terrific," she vaguely heard him say softly, chuckling as he observed the prone form that had slid silently down into the bucket seat. "Now, what?"

He scooped her out of the car, carrying her against his chest up the porch steps to her door. "Damn. Jan. Jan, honey, where's the key?"

"Ummm. Key?"

"To your door. Where's the house key, darlin'?"

She opened her eyes momentarily to glance down at the shoulder bag he'd slung around her neck. "Purse," she mumbled. Jan smiled sweetly, her eyelids fluttering closed again as she nestled closer.

Dave looked around in quiet desperation, the frown easing from his forehead as he spotted the swing in the shadows of the wide front porch. It squeaked slightly in protest, the damp sea air keeping it in constant need of oil, as he placed her limp body onto the wooden slats. Digging through the contents of her purse, he found the key he was seeking and went to open the door.

Lifting her up once again, he carried her into the house and down the short hallway to her bedroom, where he placed her onto the yellow-and-white-checked bedspread. In no time at all, he'd freed her yielding figure from the slim white jeans, the red-and-white-striped shirt, and her lacy bra. Pulling back the matching sheets, he slid her easily into bed, bending to brush her hair back from her face. He dropped a light kiss onto her cheek.

"O.K., babe," he said into her ear softly. "What time do you have to leave for the pool?"

"Ummm."

"Jan . . . work . . . morning . . . what time?" He questioned her in the same disjointed phrases she'd used earlier, pleased when it prompted a muffled response.

"Eight," she mumbled, rolling over onto her

stomach to bury her head into the soft foam of the pillow. "Eight o'clock. Morning."

"Eight o'clock," he repeated, giving her one last very long look before leaving.

Chapter Seven

۰۸

Jan brushed a limp hand at the annoying tickle teasing her skin along her shoulder blades. Rolling over and pulling the sheets over her head, she hunched deeper into the soft comfort of the mattress.

"Good morning."

The deep voice had her jerking upright in an unconscious response, arms flailing at the intruder in her dimly lit bedroom. Her sleep-glazed eyes struggled to focus as strong hands caught hers in the air, holding them above her head.

"Do you always wake up like this?" Dave swam into focus, his keen blue eyes capturing her attention first.

"Of course not!" Jan tugged to reclaim her hands. "But I usually don't wake up with a man standing over my bed, either!"

He gave a low, pleased whistle. "That's a relief. It's nice to know I'm privileged."

"Not privileged." He still hadn't released his hold on her and Jan felt extremely foolish with her arms up in the air like this. Her sudden movement had shaken the sheet down about her waist and she cast a glance downward, realizing she was quite naked and very vulnerable at the moment.

"You're simply more ill-mannered than most. Do

you usually sneak your way into a lady's bedroom like this?"

"No. I usually don't have to. More often than not, I'm invited." The blue eyes danced with devilish amusement.

"Well, you're not invited here."

"You didn't mind last night." He finally released her.

Last night? Had he been here? Lord, wouldn't she remember that?

Dave's eyes gleamed down as his white teeth flashed in a smile she was sure he used to charm people from San Diego to Timbuktu. "I put you to bed, remember? And I've returned to wake you in time for your lesson this morning. That was the truth, wasn't it? That you work today?"

Jan leaned back, lifting the pillow up against the maple headboard as she eyed him warily. "Yes. How did you know that?"

"You told me. And I agreed to come with you. So, here I am, as promised."

He certainly was, she thought, eyeing him carefully for the first time. He was wearing a short shirt, cut off across his hard, muscular torso at midpoint, exposing the arrowhead of burnished golden-red curls that disappeared into the low waistband of his white shorts. Those same shorts she'd seen him wearing the first time, alongside the road. The whipcord muscles of the tanned, bare legs were a little too much to take first thing in the morning, and Jan lifted her eyes back to his face.

Amusement lifted the corners of his mouth, a muscle twitching in the tanned cheek above it, assuring her that Dave knew of the effect he was having on her. Jan drew the sheet even tighter, as if to deny the warm tingling the man was causing in her loins. If she'd thought her legs had been wobbly last night, Dave Barrie was turning them to warm water this morning!

"Get up and get that beautiful body into some clothes," he advised. "I'll finish breakfast."

Her sleep-hazed senses had slowly begun to stir to the stimulus of the new day—jolted, she felt sure, by the assault his masculinity had created. Her nostrils flared slightly, drawing in the familiar but unexpected scent.

"Is that bacon frying?"

"Of course. Part of a nutritional breakfast." His grin tilted lazily.

Jan combed her fingers through her sleep-ruffled hair. "I don't know if I have any coffee."

"Yes, you do. I thought about it after I'd already bought the groceries. So I picked some up at McDonald's. See how easily I adjust to living with an obsessive woman? I'm even willing to supply my own food."

His long fingers reached out to tousle her hair even more, then he turned to leave the room.

"Dave?" There was hesitation in her voice.

He'd reached the doorway and turned at her soft request.

Jan's eyes were round with honest inquiry and the single query was almost indistinct in the soft morning air. "Why?"

Dave seemed completely at ease as he lounged against the door frame, folding his arms across the bared skin of his lower chest as he considered the question. His eyes viewed her across the intervening space, surveying her with gravity. Then the thoughtful appraisal was chased away by blue sparks of humor as he gave her that lazy, devastating smile.

"I told you, darlin'," he crooned softly, "I'm working on becoming your latest obsession. If I'm the last man you see before you fall asleep and the first man you see when you wake up—who knows? You may just fall into liking the pattern." He winked and left the room.

This couldn't go on! He hadn't done anything she could honestly complain about. Anything she hadn't invited, really. But the man had charged into her life with all the strength of a velvet bulldozer and taken over. Jan would have to put a stop to it! Before he *did* become a habit, an obsession.

"You don't have any egg cups." The blue eyes were lightly accusing as she entered the sunny, plant-filled kitchen.

She eyed the plate he placed on the breakfast bar. "I didn't have any eggs, either. But I don't see that stopping you."

Jan flopped down onto a bar stool at the counter. As she swiveled in his direction, their legs brushed and she jumped slightly. The contact of his hair-covered leg against hers reminded her all too vividly of another time she'd felt those same long legs over hers. He turned, and they were facing each other, knees touching under the extended countertop.

"Ouch! The lady's a dragon in the morning," he observed with an exaggerated wince. "Oh, well, it was probably unrealistic of me to expect you to be perfect. I'll just have to remember to keep my innate cheeriness and good humor in check until you've had your first cup of coffee."

The egg was cooked perfectly, which for some reason irritated her even further. "Why don't you just keep your innate cheeriness high above Mission Bay? Where you belong," she added pointedly.

"*This* is where I belong," Dave replied, seemingly unperturbed by her acid tone. "Coffee." He pushed a white styrofoam cup in her direction. "Drink. You'll feel better."

A ginger-toned brow rose as Jan dumped in the

usual two spoonfuls of sugar. "Terrible! For an athlete, the woman has horrendous eating habits!"

"Look, Mr. Healthy Body," she remarked, taking a bite of crisp golden bacon, "I've had a man who supervised every bite that went into my mouth. As you may have noticed, he's no longer around. Does that tell you anything?"

An impassive mask covered his face. "Only that you're still rebelling by not eating properly. In which case, I can only plead guilty to contributing to your delinquency."

The familiar light returned to the jeweled blue eyes as Dave reached into the bag and pulled something out. Jan grabbed at it like a greedy child, eyeing him over the wrapper, a brilliant smile on her face.

"How did you know I'm wild about chocolate bars?"

"It's hard to miss. The ashtray of your car is so stuffed with wrappers it won't close. When I climbed in that day, I told myself, Dave old boy, what you've got here is one beautiful chocolate freak. If you want to get anywhere with her, you'd better speak softly and carry a big Hershey bar."

Jan pulled off the brown wrapper, making a slow, deliberate act of self-denial as she unwrapped the white, waxed inner liner. The anticipation alone was an important part of the ritual, and she made herself take as long as physically possible. She eyed the fragrant little brown squares for a time, inhaling the heady fragrance and closing her eyes to savor the delightful messages it was sending to her brain.

The beloved aroma triggered the proper response and her mouth moistened as she reached out and broke off a single, tiny square. Dave had had the bag in his car, and the San Diego morning sun had softened the chocolate, coating her fingertips with a light sheen of the rich, dark candy.

Her tongue reached out to curl around it, the sensitive tastebuds testing and sampling with the intensity of a wine connoisseur. An expression of sheer bliss lit her expectant face, softening her features as she caught his interested study. A small smile of enchantment touched her lips and her eyes were bright as they met his reflective study.

His own eyes were lit from within as they moved to her mouth, suddenly naked with desire as he watched her tongue come out to circle her lips like the little pink tongue of a cat, drawing in any of the soft, melted chocolate that might be left there.

"Uh uh." The command was issued softly, but with authority in the caressingly low pitch as Jan moved her fingers toward her lips. Dave reached out and took her hand, his thumb making little tracing circles on her palm.

Jan felt his eyes will her gaze into his and she was caught in a smoky blue gaze that seemed to be consuming her. His eyes were deep as a storm-tossed sea as he took her fingers. One by one he put them into his own mouth, his lips closing about them to take off the smooth, melted chocolate. Jan could feel his tongue circling, gathering up the sweet candy, and the slight sucking motion of his lips was having an undeniable effect on the rest of her body.

She could feel her heartbeat quickening, her pulse racing a little faster and a little hotter as the steady movement of his tongue and lips began to spread an evocative ache from her thighs. A restless fluttering deep inside her made Jan sigh with yearning pleasure, and he heard it, his eyes registering satisfaction.

Her full, tenderly shaped lips parted slightly and Jan passed her tongue unconsciously over them, as if sharing the taste of the chocolate. Dave held her gaze by the vivid strength of his will as he continued to torment her, each finger in turn treated to the erotic cleansing. The heady sexual tension was exquisite and prolonged and her body finally betrayed her as she shivered deliciously at the intimacy the act had created.

Jan was as taut as a coiled spring, her head singing with the beat of her own blood as the treacherous tongue moved to brush against the center of her palm, following the trail his thumb had made earlier.

"There. All cleaned up."

The only consolation Jan had, as he returned her hand to her lap, was that his deep, usually controlled voice was as rough as she knew hers would be if she even attempted to speak. And his chest, under the cut-off T-shirt, was rising and falling in a rhythm that was anything but steady.

She didn't understand what he'd done, or how in the world he'd managed to do it, but like every other time, Dave had woven a spell of enchantment about them. From an experience that had always been pleasurable, he'd evoked a feeling so sensuous, so erotic, that she'd never be safe passing a candy rack again.

"I don't understand." The thought was spoken out loud, emitted on a shaken breath.

Dave had garnered control, his voice a tantalizing drawl. "I told you, darlin'. I'm working on obsessions here. I dare you to ever eat another chocolate bar without thinking of me. Without wanting me like you did a minute ago."

The color fled from her deeply tanned face. Suddenly, Jan felt totally vulnerable, devoid of any form of natural self-protection. Like a chameleon who's being stalked by a snake and suddenly discovers he's lost his ability to change color.

"You're unscrupulous." She pressed her palms together in her lap to calm their involuntary trembling. "And ruthless!"

Jan looked up at the suddenly icy color of his eyes and realized she was seeing Maggie's man of legend—the man who'd survived the network wars to remain unscathed. A man who'd overcome a background so apparently harsh that he'd been unwilling to reveal anything but bits and pieces of his past.

There was a brutal strength about him as his tawny head was thrown back to reveal the bronzed darkness of his throat when he swallowed the last of his coffee. Crushing the styrofoam in a careless gesture, Dave tossed it into her wastebasket and rose from the stool to stand over her, a sleek, satisfied smile on his face. Those crystal eyes practically shouted out his victory. There was an air of confidence about Dave Barrie that Jan had never witnessed in any other man. And suddenly, unexpectedly, a ruthlessness that boded ill will to anyone who might be foolish enough to stand in his way.

"Only when necessary, darlin'," he answered her. "Only when necessary."

Jan was silent as they walked out to the car. She'd been thrown off her guard by Dave's refusal to reestablish the physical intimacy they'd shared that incredible night. But there was a certain intimacy developing here, one far greater than that of pure physical knowledge of each other's bodies.

Little by little he was learning everything about her, infiltrating the most private aspects of her life, and it frightened her. Jan felt as if she were cliff diving with a blindfold tied over her eyes. She knew those deadly rocks were down there, knew she could end up broken on their jagged spires, but all she could do was plunge in and hope for the best.

Because she was beginning to realize that whatever happened, there was no turning back.

Dave paused before the cars parked in the driveway. "Let's take yours. It's a perfect day to put the top down."

Jan looked up at him. His blue eyes were shaded by a pair of dark-gray lenses, a concession to the brilliant California sun.

"Why are you insisting on coming with me, in the first place? Surely you've better ways to spend your day off."

"Not really." Dave shrugged. "I'm interested in seeing the other side of Jan Baxter, athlete. The one who gives up her day off and spends it working with some poor kids when there's no possible reward in it. No Olympic medals, no up-and-coming future stars to guide to fame. No money. No interviews on the evening news."

"There is a reward in it!"

Jan had silently acquiesced to his choice of cars, and moved to hers. Now she leaned against the front fender, her arms folded across her chest as she looked up into those gray lenses. She could see herself reflected in them, could see her tense, argumentative stance, which wasn't particularly attractive. But he'd managed to strike a sore spot and she wasn't going to back down gracefully. Not this time!

"Perhaps you've always been endowed with a sense of your own worth, Dave Barrie, exaggerated as it may be. But not all of us mortals are so blessed. We struggle along, hoping to find one thing we can hold on to. One thing that'll make us feel we're capable human beings who are worth something.

"If the ability to do a half-gainer off a springboard after hours of work makes a kid feel a little proud, a little rewarded by his effort, perhaps he'll feel stronger. And if that renewed strength, slight as it might be, encourages him to reach out and try something else—something a little further beyond his grasp—well, there's always a chance he might end up with the brass ring, after all. And even if he doesn't, for a short time he's felt good about himself. And *that's* the reward. No money. No medals. No publicity. Just a chance to share in the human condition."

Her hands moved down to her hips, clad in denim cut-off jeans, fists resting on the hard line of her slender hipbone. Her face was looking up into his and Jan was growing impatient because the glasses kept her from studying any expression that might be revealed in those blue eyes. It was that inability to read the emotion that had her unprepared for the red-gold head suddenly swooping down to capture her lips under his.

Jan gasped with surprise as his mouth covered hers, her breath caught in the back of her throat. His palms were placed on either side of her on the gunmetal gray of the convertible, forestalling her flight. At first, the response irked her. It was as if he'd totally disregarded her ardent declaration. Jan steeled herself, attempting to ignore the mastery of his firm lips as they plucked at the defensive closing of her own.

Dave appeared not the least bit disturbed by her hostile reaction, and the seductive movements of his lips didn't cease in their provocative caress. Her hands reached out to press against his chest and she could feel the steady beat of his heart under her fingertips. He still hadn't touched her, his hands resting on the car, but now Jan was aware of his elbows bending on either side as he leaned forward into the kiss, closing the gap between them. Her own arms were forced to bend in response, still resting on the hard chest, but now the distance between them was spanned only by her hands.

His hands moved to her waist, drawing her lower body against his, his knee moving between her bare legs. Jan gave up, finding herself arching in an instinctive, womanly response. Her hips strained up to him, her lips moved against his—no longer in protest, but in hunger—as she parted them to invite the deep exploration of his thrusting tongue into the sweet recesses of her mouth. Her hands moved to his arms, climbing to cling around his neck, straining upward as she sought to expunge any distance between them. Her body was feverish as he returned the embrace and she felt herself pressed between the sun-warmed metallic heat of the car and the male warmth of his hard body.

Jan's own body had come alive, feeling almost like a foreign territory to her, so unfamiliar were the impulses leaping along her nerve synapses. A foreign territory that at this moment yearned for a conqueror. His hands left the curving roundness of her bottom to move slowly back up her body to her shoulders, where he held her as he backed away.

"You are incredibly sexy when riled, Jan Banning Baxter," he drawled huskily. "I'll be sure to keep that in mind." Dave glanced around them at the quiet suburban neighborhood that hadn't yet come to life on this early weekend morning. The only sign of movement was a lawn service down the street, the steady whirring drone of the mower foreshadowing the bustling that would take over as people began covering the warm sands of the beach.

"And next time, before I get your dander up, I'll make certain we're in a more secluded spot. Such as that cheery, sunshine-yellow bedroom you've got in there." His tawny head jerked back in the direction of her house.

Dave then handed her the key ring he'd taken from her purse last night. "Why don't you drive, darlin', since you know the way?"

He opened the passenger door and slid his long, lanky frame into the velour seat, putting his hands behind his head as he leaned back against the head-rest. "Ready?" He grinned up at her.

"Unscrupulous," Jan muttered under her breath, slamming her body into the driver's seat and twisting the key with a vicious motion. Dave's head turned toward her as she pulled out of the driveway with an angry roar of the engine, but the wide gray lenses were impenetrable. Jan could, however, feel the teasing light dancing in those hidden blue eyes. The man toyed with her! Like a very well-fed cat playing with a mouse.

"I'm not," she muttered, slowing down as she approached the red-and-white hexagon stop sign.

"Not what?"

Jan glared at the sunglasses. "I'm not your damn catnip mouse!"

A chuckle rumbled from his muscled chest as he reached over, his fingertips massaging the back of her neck with an easy, familiar gesture. "Oh, honey, do I ever know that."

"Then stop playing with me as if I am!"

Dave's free hand moved up to his face to yank off the glasses, the hand on the back of her neck reaching to turn her face toward him as they idled at the stop sign, waiting for a truckload of Imperial Valley lettuce to lumber across the intersection. The unshielded eyes were a stormy, deepening blue, the pupils shrinking to black ink spots as they narrowed to shut out the sudden glare of the sun.

"I'm not playing, Jan. Believe it."

She stared helplessly into the intense, warning gaze, jumping when the car horn behind them sounded. Wrenching her eyes away from his, Jan looked up to see that the truck had passed. With an apologetic wave to the car behind her, she pulled into the intersection, returning her rather shaky attention to the road.

Chapter Eight

Jan drove to an older section of the county, pulling into a parking lot that was dotted with deep pot-holes. Avoiding them as if she were on a well-traveled obstacle course, she pulled the car into a barely defined spot. So many white diagonal lines had been painted on the fractured asphalt over the years that it was difficult to determine which were the proper ones to use, but Jan came here with enough frequency to recognize the accepted spaces.

Dave climbed out of the car, his gaze sweeping the vast assortment of cars already in the lot. If anyone thought the roads were too crowded with imports these days, this lot would be a revelation. Detroit's heyday was represented right here. The place was cluttered with battleship-size, battered old Chevrolets, Fords, and Dodges, punctuated here and there by a pickup that had been given a new coat of paint via a spray can. Overspray drifted across windshields and tires.

In a far corner of the lot, as if holding a convention, there was a group of vividly remodeled low-riders, their chrome trim and lavishly customized paint gleaming in the sunshine.

"A man's car is his castle," she said with a smile, following Dave's gaze to the cars, which were in various states of individualization. The pleated and rolled crushed-velvet upholstery and welded-chain steering wheels seemed to be standard equipment.

"Aren't you worried about getting this car ripped off around here?"

Jan shook her dark head. "Uh uh. They all know me. I've been working here about five years. The only thing I lose is a battery, periodically. It takes twelve good-sized batteries to work the hydraulic lifts on those things. Every so often I come out and discover some kid has borrowed mine. But it's usually a new kid, so I don't worry about it. I just put the word out and, poof, little gremlins return it. Safe and sound."

Dave eyed her thoughtfully as they made their way across the parking lot. She saw something stirring in his studied appraisal, piquing the sensation of butterflies in her stomach fluttering their papery wings. Suddenly it seemed vitally important for her to know what he was thinking about her.

It was a disquieting thought, realizing that she actually cared—desperately. She ran her tongue over lips that had gone strangely dry, and her confused green gaze was swallowed by the drawn intentness of his eyes. Her breath was trapped in her throat, refusing to allow the question her mind was screaming. What did Dave think of her? And, even more important, what did he want of her?

He rubbed his jaw thoughtfully, prolonging the agonizing study. Then, when Jan was certain that her nerves had frayed to the snapping point, he gave a slight nod of his head.

"I'll meet you out by the pool," he said in a voice that belied the electricity that had been arcing between them for—how long? A few seconds? Minutes? It could have been an eternity, Jan thought, the way he'd removed them both from the physical realm of time and space.

"Sure," she mumbled, watching as he paid the

cashier his money and disappeared into the men's dressing room. He hadn't touched her, hadn't said a word. Yet, in that ethereal space of time he had left Jan feeling as if she'd been buffeted by gale-force winds.

Jan almost choked on an intake of breath as she watched Dave make his way toward her. Tall and rangy, he moved with athletic grace, as if totally unaware of the many pairs of female eyes watching his long strides. She felt she should have been prepared. I've seen the man naked, for heaven's sake, she thought. But just like that first time, his body was a shock.

Somehow, seeing him barely clad in the shimmery rust-colored swim trunks that only served to draw attention to his uncompromising maleness, Jan felt even more of a shock. The white towel draped loosely about his shoulders contrasted with his dark-gold skin; Dave Barrie was a compelling masculine figure.

He reached her side and was looking down at her with a lopsided grin, appearing as affable as a puppy. "All ready for a day of watching you share in the human condition."

She wasn't to be taken in that easily. "You're crazy." Jan shook her head as she started toward the deep end of the pool, where her kids were waiting.

Dave fell in step beside her, still grinning. "So are you, remember? That's why we make such a terrific team."

"Hey, Jan!" This came from a chubby teenage girl, her wet hair sprung into long corkscrew curls. "Who's the hunk?"

"Hey! I'm a hunk." He sounded pleased.

"Don't let it go to your head," she advised dryly. "Alice has never been known to be terribly choosy about her male friends."

"How about the teacher? Is she choosy?"

"Extremely."

Dave stopped, his hands gripping the ends of the white towel as he tugged it back and forth. Jan was brought to a halt as she realized he was no longer beside her, and she turned, eyeing him questioningly over her shoulder.

Blue eyes danced merrily. "Well?"

"Well, what?"

"Does the teacher think I'm a hunk?"

Jan fought the smile tugging the corners of her lips as she viewed the almost-boyish appeal on his face. All that sweet charm hid so much dangerous steel. Her shoulders lifted and dropped in a slight sigh of resignation.

"The teacher thinks you're a hunk," she agreed, allowing the smile to bloom like a full-blown summer rose. "Now, can she get to work?"

"I won't say another word," he promised, lowering himself down onto the broken-edged coping and dangling his feet into the turquoise depths.

After an initial rowdiness, due to Dave's unexpected appearance, the kids settled down to work. It didn't help that they all recognized him immediately. Once again, Jan felt like some alien being newly arrived on the planet earth. Dave shrugged his shoulders, giving her a slightly sheepish grin.

They were a mixed group, ranging in age from seven to seventeen. Mario, the eldest, had potential, Jan thought as she watched his dark, muscular body fly off the high dive for the umpteenth time. If she were forced to pick a favorite out of all the students she'd taught, Mario would probably rank at the top of the list.

Given different circumstances of birth, he might have been one of her pupils at the club. But his was not the life of a child whose parents had the money to pursue years of expensive training. And he was certainly not of the social peer group who'd be impressed by his skills.

Mario worked in order to support his mother and five younger brothers and sisters. The Olympics to him was just another sports show that turned up on his television set every four years. But Mario had a goal. He wanted to cliff-dive in Acapulco. It was a goal he worked for with as much energy as Jan herself had ever worked toward Munich. More, she acknowledged. He'd had to overcome so many more barriers.

As such, they understood each other—even respected each other. With him as the unofficial leader of the class, Jan had never experienced a moment's discipline problem. Mario knew just when to apply a well-chosen word. Not the word Jan might have chosen herself—but infinitely more effective.

Jan knew that Mario worked as a box boy at an all-night grocery, and the late hours were definitely showing in his dives. Something just wasn't clicking today. Instead of the usual clean entry, the water was splashing up in a wide spray. He began to fling himself off the three-meter board, which extended out ten feet over the glistening blue surface of the water with a vengeance. The angrier and more frustrated he became, the harder he propelled his body into the pool, and the wider and harsher the splash. Finally, after a particularly virulent string of Spanish oaths, he stalked to the exit, his head held as high as any conquistador. The good-natured teasing dropped off immediately and there was absolute silence as everyone watched their leader stalk from the pool. The only sound was the water lapping against the stained blue and white tiles.

Jan knew the feeling. She knew how some days it seemed that nothing could go right, no matter how hard you tried. But Mario had his pride to think about, and if she allowed him to leave today, returning next week would be more difficult for him. The prospect that there might not be a next time for him was dismal, and he'd worked too hard to give up now. She'd worked too hard with him!

She didn't run after him, but her stride was long and purposeful as she caught up with him right outside the gate. Mario shook off her arm, but he didn't leave and the poolside observers had a ringside seat as Jan violently shook her head at every argument Mario was obviously offering. Then it was her turn, and her expression was as firm and unyielding as a concrete wall. Mario turned his back on her, arms crossed on his dark, steely chest. Undaunted, Jan continued until finally she had him turning slightly to look over his shoulder at something she'd said.

Jan grinned, her smile cracking the hard lines of her face, and it was returned hesitantly. She held out a slim hand, waiting patiently. There was a collective sigh of relief as the gesture was accepted and Mario shook her outstretched hand, returning to the diving area with her.

This time it was Jan who climbed the ladder to the board. She thought, on his last dive, that she'd noticed Mario pulling his arms back too far as he left the board. He'd reluctantly agreed to watch a demonstration and try again. Jan could only pray that she was right.

She moved out onto the springy board with all the inherent grace of a ballerina. Then, after a moment's contemplation, she executed the dive with fine precision, her arms outstretched in a line with her shoulders in midair, bringing them together above her head in a straight line with her body just before she entered the water. She was nearly in line with the board, her body at right angles to the surface of the water as she cut into it like a newly sharpened knife, leaving barely a ripple in her wake. She bobbed to the surface and levered herself out of the pool. She spoke in an undertone to Mario, and her arms gestured as she held them out, first pulled back, then in the proper position—a straight line with her shoulders.

The young man nodded grimly and began the long climb up the ten-foot ladder. Jan, acknowledging Dave's presence for the first time since she'd begun the class, came to sit beside him, dangling her feet next to his in the water. Almost unconsciously, her hand inched its way along the coping to slip into his. By the time Mario had reached the top rung, her fingernails were digging into Dave's skin, and if she was breathing, it would have been impossible to tell. All eyes were raised upward.

As Mario broke the surface of the water, after a perfect duplication of Jan's dive, she turned to Dave, her face wreathed with a breathtaking smile, her eyes glistened with unshed tears.

"I understand."

That was all Dave said as they drove away, this time with him handling the driving chores. Jan felt terrific. She felt good not only because Mario would someday reach his goal—she knew that without the slightest doubt—but also because he'd learned something important about himself today.

Mostly, however, she felt terrific because she was sitting in this car, the friendly California sun baking down on her skin, next to a man whose company she enjoyed more than anyone she'd ever known. She smiled. No words were necessary.

Dave Barrie's self-control seemed to take over completely as he arrived at her door each morning, bearing a breakfast that he would cook and insist

she eat. At lunch he'd show up at the club to whisk
her off for a picnic somewhere—on the beach or in
the lush atmosphere of Balboa Park. He was careful
not to keep her away from the club for too long, so
James Waring couldn't fault her behavior,
although Jan noted that the president of the club
had taken to grinding his teeth as Dave sauntered
into view each day.

It was as if Dave were determined to fill her life
with him, and Jan was becoming more and more
uneasy as she discovered herself looking forward to
seeing him. There was such a thin line between
anticipating his arrival and becoming dependent
on it.

"You have to stop coming over every evening,"
she told him one night, watching him gather the
makings for an enormous cheeseburger. All he
wanted to do with her anymore was feed her!
"You're ruining my running schedule, and with all
this food you keep shoving down me, I'll be the size
of the Goodyear blimp before long. I'll empty the
pool when I dive."

"Running?" He mixed a sauce of salad dressing,
catsup, and pickle relish, holding out a spoonful for
her to taste.

"Good," she agreed, momentarily sidetracked.
Then she jumped the detour and returned the conversation to her original track. "I used to run on the
beach every night. Now I don't."

"O.K.," he agreed cheerfully as he placed an out-
rageously large slice of Spanish onion on each
toasted bun. "Dinner's ready."

O.K.? What kind of reaction was that? He hadn't
even put up the argument she'd been preparing for
since three o'clock that afternoon.

The next evening Jan paced the floor of her house
like a caged lion, her head spinning toward the
window at the sound of each car passing out front.

Finally, as she watched the setting sun gilding the water of the Pacific Ocean with a ruby, gold, and amethyst glow, she decided Dave wasn't coming. She'd gotten her wish, hadn't she? Wasn't this what she wanted?

She was running along the hard-packed sand close to the water's edge when she heard the steady pounding of footfalls behind her. As the owner drew up, Jan glanced over, knowing in advance whom she'd see. That magical, devastating grin greeted her as Dave matched his stride to hers, his long legs extending from the navy shorts and moving as if in tandem with her own.

"What are we doing here?" Jan looked around the parking lot filled with cars.

"Seeing that you're well taken care of." Dave slid the keys into his jeans pocket and dropped a quick peck onto her lips. She could have shot him as he pulled away far too quickly. It was getting incredibly frustrating. Ever since that bleak experience in his penthouse apartment, these light, platonic kisses were all she'd received from him. Jan was all in favor of self-discipline, but the man was definitely carrying things to the extreme.

She folded her arms across her chest, glaring at him. "There are a lot of better ways to do that than feed me, Dave Barrie."

He laughed, reading the frustrated yearning written all over her face. "Tell me you love me," he said, "and I'll turn this car around right now and take you home with me."

"You're incredibly stubborn."

"So are you, babe. But those are my terms."

"I need time, Dave. I told you that."

"Fine. You'll have it. I'm going away for a while."

Her eyes flew to his face, distress paling her skin under her deep tan. "Where?"

Dave smiled, reaching out to ruffle her hair. "Sacramento. For three days, that's all."

The laughter vanished from his eyes as his hand cupped the back of her head, drawing her to him for a long, breathless kiss. It had been so long! Jan ran her hands through his soft, gingery hair, oblivious to the interested stares from passersby as she lost herself to the magic of being wrapped in his strong arms once again.

"Three days," he said unsteadily as they drew apart. "After that, I'm taking the decision out of your hands. No more kid gloves for you, lady. . . . Now, come with me." He opened the car door.

"What are we doing?"

"I told you, woman. I'm going away." He pointed in the direction of the supermarket. "See that big brick building with the wide glass windows filled with pretty signs? That, my undomestic darling, is a grocery store. We're going shopping. I'm filling Mother Hubbard's cupboards before I leave tonight. I want all those womanly curves right where they belong when I get back." He slanted a wicked grin in her direction. "And you can take my word for it that I've every intention of checking to see that they're still there. Inch by perfect inch."

Dave began putting away the groceries, as familiar with Jan's kitchen as with his own. She perched on a barstool, preparing to watch the videotape of the news. True to his word, Dave had shown up one evening with the recorder, and although she'd protested, Jan had to admit she looked forward to watching him each evening. His series on sports and drugs had been well done, so far. While revealing some discomforting facts, he'd veered away from the sensationalism some reporters might have resorted to in order to boost the ratings.

"Do you need any help?" she asked over her shoulder.

"Nope. Go ahead and watch. I've got everything under control. But first I think I should tell you something—"

"Hush," she instructed as the commercial faded from the screen, "my favorite newsman is coming on."

Jan turned her attention back to the screen, experiencing again that warm rush of emotion she felt whenever she watched him. She didn't know how it had happened, or when, but Dave Barrie had become an intrinsic part of her life. She loved him, she realized, sharing her loving gaze between the man on her television screen and the living version at work in her kitchen.

Then her heart stopped beating. She was vaguely aware of Dave standing behind her, all domestic chores halted for the moment. James Waring was on the screen, assuring Dave that there had never been, in his tenure of office, any drugs at La Conquista. Jan was further shocked to see footage of herself demonstrating a dive as Dave's voice-over promised to compare the attitude toward drugs at one of the city's most exclusive clubs with that of one more humble. With that teaser for tomorrow's report, Jan wasn't surprised to see the camera panning the parking lot of the Diablo public pool.

"Well?" he asked quietly.

She turned toward him. "How did you get that film of me?"

He shrugged. "It was in the tape library at the station. I thought putting a pretty woman in might spice things up a bit. Otherwise it would've been just another interview with a boring, self-serving individual who prefers to keep his head buried in the sand. How can you work for that guy, anyway? He's a real creep."

Despite her agreement, Jan refused to make light of his latest report. Dave seemed to be attempting to avoid direct confrontation as he began his kitchen chores once again.

She slid off the stool, reaching out to take the box of cereal from his hand. "Stop putting those damn groceries away and explain that," she snapped, slamming the corn flakes onto the counter.

"Explain why I think James Waring the Third is a twenty-four-carat phony? Or how your two pools ended up on my series?"

"The latter. I don't very much care how you feel toward James Waring, Dave, he's my business."

"I know," he growled, his expression harsh as he got the cereal put away in the cupboard. "And from the way he looks at you every time we go to lunch, I'd say he'd like to make you *his* business."

"Dammit, Dave. I want to talk about this. Why didn't you tell me what you were doing?"

"I was going to, Jan. I just wanted to wait until I was close to wrapping everything up. That's why I wanted to talk to you before you watched it tonight. I've been following this trail and—"

"And it leads to El Diablo?"

"No. Not there."

Her eyes widened. "Are you telling me your so-called trail leads to someone at La Conquista?"

For the first time since she'd known him, Dave Barrie seemed terribly uncomfortable. This wasn't going as smoothly as he'd planned it, Jan realized. Because she wasn't the pushover he'd assumed her to be.

He had the grace to turn away from her accusatory glare, reaching into the paper bag to withdraw the frozen foods. "It seems to, Jan."

"Seems to? You don't know?"

"I know," he mumbled, continuing to work.

Jan grabbed the Cornish game hen from his hand, throwing it onto the counter. The frozen bird skidded across the green Formica, scattering food to the floor.

"You've been using me, haven't you? You've been following me around—to the club, to El Diablo—pretending that you cared for me. All that just to get your damn story!"

"You're dead wrong, Jan." Dave's voice was like cold steel. "And I resent even the implication that I'd do that." His irritated gaze took in the mess she'd made of the kitchen. "Now, if you don't mind, I think I'll finish putting these things away."

"I do mind!" Jan picked up the carton of eggs, slamming them to the floor along with the other groceries, feeling a foolish surge of retribution as she watched the gooey mess ooze out over his shoes. "And you've got a lot of nerve talking about what you resent. Let me tell you what I resent, Dave Barrie!"

All the pain surfaced as Jan realized how near she'd been to declaring her love for this man. This traitor. Her finger jabbed against his chest as her voice rose to an unnaturally high pitch.

"I resent the fact that you lied to me. That you let me believe you loved me in order to boost your standings enough to win some damn anchor spot. I resent the fact that you didn't just come right out and ask for my help. I would have, you know. If you really have reason to believe my kids are using drugs, then I had the right to know. So why didn't you just ask me?"

"Jan, listen to me—"

Suddenly a horrible thought occurred to her, and she sank back onto the chair, all the fight drained from her as icy fingers clutched her heart.

"You thought it might be me, didn't you? That's

why you didn't say anything. That's what all this sticking to me like glue has been about. You think I'm doping the kids to win an Olympic berth."

Dave shook his head, moving to put both hands on her shoulders. "Jan, that isn't true. You're overreacting to all this."

"Get out, Dave."

"Babe, we've got to talk this out before I go."

"I trusted you. Why couldn't you have trusted me?"

"Dammit, Jan, you're not listening!"

"I've listened to everything you could possibly say that would make a difference, Dave. Now, please, just leave me alone."

He appraised her intently, seeming to want to continue the conversation. Then, as if deciding there wasn't much point, he bent down to pick up the egg carton and put it into the sink.

"I'll call you from Sacramento," he said softly.

"Don't bother."

"It's no bother."

"I won't answer the phone."

He paused in the doorway. "Yes, you will," he decided, leaving her alone for the time being.

Jan slumped in the chair, trying to remember if she'd ever felt so terrible in her entire life. Her bleak tourmaline gaze moved around the kitchen. The room looked as though a tornado had torn through the place, leaving nothing but rubble in its path. It resembled her life at the moment—an absolute shambles.

Chapter Nine

For the first time she could remember, Jan called in sick. She stayed in bed for hours, reviewing the harsh accusation she'd flung at Dave over and over again. If only she'd been willing to listen to his explanation . . .

And what do you think he would've said? an argumentative little voice in the back of her mind asked.

I don't know, she admitted. But he must have had a good reason for not telling me sooner.

Sure. He thought you were mixed up in it.

"No," Jan said aloud, throwing back the covers and finally getting out of bed. "I thought that one up. Whatever else Dave thought he was doing, he doesn't believe I'm involved. I know it."

She went into the kitchen, eyeing the mess that was still scattered over the counter and the floor.

"I should've at least let him hang around long enough to clean this up," she muttered, scraping the hardened egg yolk with a spatula.

By the time the sun had set and Jan had spent her first day in weeks without him, her worst fears had come home to her. She missed him, terribly. She knew it was only three days, but they stretched ahead of her like the arid Sahara Desert—bleak and desolate. If he'd only call like he'd promised, she'd listen to anything he had to say. She loved him and wanted desperately to believe him.

Jan stared at the kitchen wall phone, her gaze locked on the bright-yellow instrument as if she could command it to ring by sheer telepathy. She was startled when the shrill bell responded, shattering her intense concentration.

"Hi," she answered somewhat breathlessly.

"Hi, yourself." Dave's deep voice, rumbling like the tide, made her warm in response. "Is it safe? Or have you figured out a way to throw things through telephone lines?"

"I'm sorry about that, Dave."

"Not as sorry as I am. I handled it miserably. Believe it or not, I was trying to protect you, honey. I'd always planned to tell you as soon as I had something definite. I still will."

His vibrant voice offered up the explanation and Jan didn't want to notice that he hadn't really shed any light on the problem. She didn't want to force herself to acknowledge that shadow of doubt hovering in her mind.

"Maggie warned me you were always right on top of a fastbreaking story," she said, grasping at any straw.

"I do seem to run into my share of incredible coincidences, darlin'. And believe me, that's all it was in your case."

"You can't tell me who you suspect? It's my club."

"Honey, I've got to protect my sources. And at this point, it's still only conjecture. Just trust me, O.K.?"

"O.K., Dave. I will." I want to anyway, Jan added silently.

"Good. Are you all right? I called the club today and they said you hadn't come in."

"I'm fine. I was just tired."

"Are you eating?"

"Not yet."

"But you will."

She sighed. "Of course. Is that all you care about? Feeding me?"

"No, I've been fattening you up for my own nefarious purposes, my dear. Wait until I get home."

The light, teasing tone banished the lingering problem, and Jan laughed softly. "Sure. Just like the wicked witch in *Hansel and Gretel*."

"Smart girl. And well-read."

"How are you?" Jan asked softly, clinging to the phone as if were Dave Barrie himself.

"As fine as I can be under the circumstances. You know, a very strange thing happened to me today."

"Oh?"

"Very strange," he repeated. "I was checking into my room, and Arthur—he's the bellman—had just demonstrated the air-conditioning and the television controls, assuring me of his availability should I need anything, before he departed with his generous tip. Then, right out of the blue it happened."

"What?"

"I missed a certain obsessive, stubborn diving instructor. There I was, alone in a hotel room for probably the millionth time in my life, and for the very first time, I was lonely." His deep voice held a slightly incredible note. "What do you think about that?"

Jan thought it was wonderful. And she thought it was horrible. He'd be spending his life in hotel rooms again all too soon, and she wouldn't be there with him. What kind of future could they possibly have together?

"I don't know," she whispered into the receiver, grateful that Dave couldn't see the bleak and miserable face that stared back from the shiny depths of a copper canister on the counter.

"I think it's going to be a rough few days," he answered his own question.

Amen. "It's your job," she said, instead.

"Yeah. But maybe not for long. Hey! Guess what? I had a call from the network not five minutes after I arrived here."

Jan tried to answer, but the painful knot in her throat blocked any form of communication except the nod of her head, which proved ineffective across the long-distance wires.

"Jan? Are you still there?"

She nodded again, clearing her throat and forcing out a weak "Yes."

"You'll never guess. They've offered me a new program. Same concept as the cable deal with tons more money. Only joker in the deck is that it'd be taped in the New York studios."

She heard it. She knew she had. Jan stared down at the telephone receiver clutched in her sweaty hand. Did Dave Barrie realize he'd just broken her heart, shattering it into a million brittle pieces all over the green-and-gold no-wax kitchen floor? Did he? Jan tried to think of something to say, her mind whirling with possibilities, all of them displaying all too blatantly her overwhelming need for him to stay here in San Diego, with her.

"Jan? There's someone at the door, probably room service with dinner. I'll call you tomorrow night, babe. O.K.?"

"O.K. Good-bye, Dave."

Jan heard his distant farewell as she returned the receiver to its wall cradle.

She'd been working everyone too hard today, Jan

realized as she left the pool for a moment to take a telephone call. She could see the exhaustion etched on every face as young bodies flopped onto the decking surrounding the Olympic-size pool. She was taking it out on them, making them tackle the same dives over and over again because misery loved company. Pure and simple. When what she *really* wanted to do was drag Barrie back from Sacramento and tie him up and keep him to herself. Forever.

The mental image of Dave tied to the four posters of her bed produced a smile on her lips as she picked up the receiver.

"Hi, Jan? Bob Bradley. I was just calling to see if you'd be able to get away for an hour or so this afternoon."

Bob Bradley was the director of the youth program at El Diablo and the two of them had been working for some time to acquire the funds to expand the swimming and diving program to the other public pools in the area.

"Gee, Bob, under normal circumstances, I would. But it's really a madhouse around here today."

Liar. The only problem you have is that you're taking out your frustrations on those poor kids, a mocking voice echoed in her brain.

"I understand," he interjected swiftly. "How about dinner? I'd really like to talk with you as soon as possible."

How about dinner? She'd only sit around an empty house, waiting for Dave's call. Then, when it came, she'd only feel worse, afraid their relationship was rapidly reaching the end of a breathtakingly thrilling roller-coaster ride. Jan knew he'd take the network offer.

Newsworld had said he was making a power play for an anchor position. And try as she might, Jan couldn't get that disquieting, ruthless other side of the man completely out of her mind. Well, that Dave Barrie had played his hand well, getting exactly what he'd wanted. She sighed, wondering how much time they had left together. The thought was so depressing she made her decision.

"That would be fine. Do you still have my address?"

"Just a sec." Jan could hear him flipping through his index file. "Got it. Still on Coronado, right?"

"Right. About seven?"

"Great. See you then. And, Jan, thanks for the time."

"No problem, Bob," she answered, curious at his expectant attitude. "I'm looking forward to it."

By the time five-thirty rolled around, Jan was feeling like the Wicked Witch of the West, so she decided the smartest thing to do would be to call it a day.

"O.K., you goldbricks," she called out, "hit the showers. We'll start fresh tomorrow."

There was a collective cheer of relief at the sudden, unexpected parole as teenagers scattered, obviously afraid she'd change her mind.

Jan was ready when Bob Bradley arrived at her house and they walked the few short blocks to the Boat House Restaurant on Glorietta Bay. The Coronado marina was one of San Diego's outstanding docking facilities, the quaint white building originally constructed to serve as a boathouse for the patrons of the elegant Hotel del Coronado across the street. Now, however, jutting out over the clear blue bay, it specialized in a delightful variety of steaks and seafood dishes.

"You look beautiful, as ever," Bob stated over cocktails, a Scotch for him, a glass of burgundy for

Jan. His dark eyes paid her compliments as they
took in her sun-bleached dark hair and her honey-
gold complexion, which was complimented by the
pastel tones of the ivory silk dress she was wearing.

"Thank you."

Pleased as she was, Jan was sorry to realize his
compliment hadn't stirred her. Dave Barrie, just by
looking at her appreciatively, could make her
melt like butter under a hot knife. Is this what the
rest of her life was going to be like? Comparing
everything to him? Every*one* to him?

"What's this all about? Not that I don't love the
opportunity to have dinner with an attractive
man."

"We've acquired enough capital for the program.
Two local soft-drink bottlers have agreed to under-
write the costs of the deal. For a little community
recognition, of course," he tacked on, grinning as
he dropped his good news in her lap.

"Of course." Jan nodded. She'd worked in the
volunteer program long enough to know that funds
were seldom given out of pure altruism; everyone
expected some type of return on their investments.
But the recreation program had been a dream for so
long. To discover it would finally come to fruition
was exciting.

"I'm so pleased." She smiled as she raised her
glass in a toast to him. "Congratulations. But I
don't understand. Do you still want me to teach at
El Diablo on Sundays? Or"—her smile widened—
"have you invited me out to give me the boot?"

"Of course I'd like you to stay on at El Diablo, if
you want," he answered swiftly. "The kids all love
you and you've worked wonders. But what I really
want to ask you is whether or not you'd be willing
to accept the position of administrator for the proj-
ect. I know I can get council approval, since no city

funds will be going toward either your salary or the expanded pool hours and the instructors."

Jan toyed with her wineglass, twirling the long crystal stem and watching the play of lights in the ruby liquid.

"Oh, Bob, I don't see how I'd have time, with the club and all."

His winning smile was just barely apologetic. "That's the tough part, Jan. This would have to be *instead* of the club. Not along with. I know how important the upcoming Olympics are to you, but in the last few years I've detected something else."

Jan's fingers ran along the rim of the glass as she gazed out across the bay. The lights had turned on along the sweeping expanse of the bridge, and it was reflected in the midnight depths of the quietly lapping water.

"What's that?" she asked softly.

Bob Bradley eyed her intently, brown eyes somber. "Your recognition of the importance of things other than monetary gain and recognition. You're a natural with these kids, Jan, and you've been a great influence in their lives. I think you know the long-lasting implications of that."

As compared to the fleeting taste of quicksilver fame? But, to give up the club . . .

"How much is the salary, Bob?"

He quoted her an amount below what she was presently earning. "We can offer you a year's contract, Jan. With longer terms as funding becomes available."

The money wasn't the problem. Jan received a check each month from her grandfather's estate that gave her quite a satisfactory income, even if she'd chosen not to work at all. The drop in pay wasn't really a consideration.

But a year! She'd never had a contract with the

club. Just an understanding that as long as everyone was happy with one another, things would remain as they were. Jan had never worried about job security, since she knew her reputation would guarantee her a spot anywhere in the country. A year was a long commitment, especially at a time when she was trying to avoid commitments. It seemed that suddenly everyone was expecting her to come up with answers, when just a few weeks ago, she hadn't even known the questions.

It would be a challenge. Heaven knows, she'd be needing something to throw herself into when Dave took off for New York, or Outer Mongolia, or wherever he'd be disappearing to. It would help fill the deep void she knew he'd leave in her life. She needn't worry about deserting her students at the club, either. With the funds available for hiring a coach at La Conquista, they'd have their pick of the best in the country.

Bob watched the play of expressions cross Jan's face, apparently knowing when to keep quiet.

"Let me think about it for a few days, can you, Bob?"

He nodded his head. "Of course. Ready to order?" The look he flashed her was brilliant, and totally satisfied.

"Where in the hell have you been?"

The phone had been ringing when Jan walked in the door, and she'd managed to catch it before it stopped.

"Out. And don't yell at me that way, Dave Barrie!"

"Do you realize I've been calling you every ten minutes for the past three hours?"

"Having been out," Jan retorted, "it would stand to reason that I'd have no way of knowing that. I'm not psychic."

"Who were you out with? Were you at your parents'?"

"No."

"No? There was a first part to that question, Jan."

"I'm well aware of that. I just don't see that it's any of your business, that's all."

"What are you wearing?"

The question caught her off guard, coming from left field like it did, and Jan answered promptly. "My ivory silk dress. Why?" She added the question suspiciously.

"You weren't out eating pizza with Maggie in an expensive little frock like that," he decided. "Where were you?"

"Are you jealous?" The sudden thought struck Jan as bizarre, but rather nice, really.

"You're damn right I am," the roar came over the telephone. "And if you don't give me some straight answers, I'll be on your doorstep within two hours, to force them from you."

"Are you threatening me?"

"Ve have vays of making you talk," he replied in a singsong tone. "And ze longer I am avay from you, ze more delightful zey are sounding."

"You're impossible." Jan laughed, her irritation dissolving like sugar crystals in hot tea. "I was out with Bob Bradley."

"Hmm. Good-looking guy. Nice guy, too. But he's asking to have a minicam dropped onto his blond head."

"Don't you dare! He offered me a job."

"A job? With money?"

"That's what most jobs of my experience pay," Jan said dryly. "I've yet to be asked to perform for dead fish."

"Touchy tonight, aren't we, sweetheart? Could it

be you're pining away for my scintillating company?"

"*Pining?* Who watches those newscasts of yours? Queen Victoria? That expression went out with hoopskirts."

"You're ducking the question. If you're not more cooperative, I'll have to send out the heavy artillery. How would you like Mike Wallace or Geraldo Rivera to show up and extract a confession from you?"

"Now, them I've heard of," Jan replied with saccharine sweetness. "They must be ever so much more famous than you."

"You know," Dave growled softly into her ear over the long-distance wire, "you're just asking to have that creamy white behind of yours blistered to a brilliant shade of scarlet."

"My goodness! Is that how they go about getting those marvelous exposés? No wonder they're so popular. I had no idea the news business was so kinky."

"You're kinky. And crazy. I've also decided you're driving me crazy."

"Well, don't bother packing your jammies and toothbrush, darling. Because it will be a very short trip."

"Jan?" The jesting tone had suddenly been replaced with a low caress that gave birth to a lump in her throat.

"Yes?"

"I miss you, honey. No joke."

Tears sprang unbidden. "I miss you, too, Dave."

"Even when you're out with other men, being wined and dined at the taxpayers' expense?"

"Especially then," she whispered, a ragged edge to her voice.

"Just what I wanted to hear, babe. Now that

we've got that settled, want to tell me about this job offer?"

There was a long, pregnant silence on the other end after Jan related her news. She wished she could see his face. What was he thinking? Dave's tone, when he answered, was newsman professional, belying any involvement.

"What did you tell him?"

"That I needed time. What do you think I should do?"

Again that little pool of silence.

"You've been making your own decisions for some time now, Jan," he said finally. "I think it's best that you continue."

His vague, noncommittal answer served to make her feel both flattered and miserable. Flattered that he realized it could only be her decision to make, that she would have to be the one to live with it, and miserable that Dave hadn't just come out and told her she couldn't take it. In a way she wanted to hear him say that she was coming to New York with him, whether she liked it or not.

But would she accept such caveman tactics? No, Jan answered herself honestly.

"Sleep on it," the deep voice advised. "Things always look clearer in the morning. . . . You know, I wish you'd already gone to bed."

"Why?"

A provocative leer entered his bass voice. "Then you'd be all snuggled between pretty yellow-checked sheets and I could pretend my lips were against that lovely little ear instead of a cold, plastic telephone receiver."

Jan fought against the trembling response of her heart. "Hunting a little rough in Sacramento? I'd think with all those government secretaries, it'd be like shooting ducks in a barrel."

"I haven't been looking," Dave said simply. "I've

already drawn a bead on my quarry, Jan Banning Baxter. . . . God, I miss you!" The last was uttered on a deep growl that caused liquid fire to leap in her veins.

"Not as much as I miss you," Jan answered honestly.

"We'll fight it out when I get home tomorrow night," Dave promised. "How are you at wrestling? Two out of three pins?"

"At least," Jan agreed breathlessly. "What time?"

"I'll be at your place by six. Can you take off a little early?"

"Of course. And Dave . . ." Her voice drifted off.

"Yeah, honey?"

"I really have missed you."

"Me too, babe. Me too."

They hung up and Jan wondered at the sudden urge she'd had to tell him that she loved him. A full, feminine smile curved her lips as she wrapped her arms tightly about herself. That would come later. Tomorrow night. In person.

Her kids practically snapped to attention the next day as she walked up, and Jan realized once again that she'd really worked everyone into a frenzy with her ill temper. Oh, well, she'd let them off early this afternoon. That would help make up for it.

"Jan?"

The footsteps were running to catch up with her, and she turned to greet James Waring.

"Good morning, Mr. Waring." Jan gave him a brilliant smile. Today Dave was coming home. Today the birds were singing, the sun was shining, and she felt absolutely giddy. Now *this* was how love was supposed to feel!

"Jan," he repeated her name, this time as a greeting, nodding the silvery head. "Could I see you this morning after you've begun workouts? In my office?"

She quickly scanned the bronzed face for signs of trouble. One thing she wasn't up to today was another jogathon around his office.

"It's business," he said curtly, as if to answer her unspoken question.

"Of course," she agreed, as if she'd never thought otherwise. "I'll see you around ten. If that's all right?"

"Fine," he agreed readily. Then a sly look crossed his self-indulgent features. "Unless you'd prefer I have a nice little lunch sent in? We could mix our business with a little pleasure."

"Ten o'clock," Jan repeated as she ran off toward the locker room, hoping she appeared to be hurrying off to work and not running away from him, which was exactly what she was doing.

It wasn't that she was afraid of him, she considered as she peeled off her clothing and slid into the red nylon tank suit. It was that she was afraid of herself and what she might do. The thought of bodily tossing Mr. James Waring III into the pool and holding him under was appearing more attractive everyday. Not until he drowned, of course. Just long enough to scare the living daylights out of the old creep!

"Ah, Jan. Come in." James Waring welcomed her, turning his wrist to observe a gold Rolex watch. "Prompt as always. Unusual trait in a woman."

His eyes took on a hungry gleam as they subjected her body to a slow, merciless tour. She'd tied a towel about her waist before leaving the pool, but Jan could feel the gray eyes honing in on her breasts and she damned the hot flush that appeared in her exposed cleavage.

"But you've always been a most unusual woman," he continued silkily.

"Why did you call me here today, Mr. Waring?" Jan forced herself to remain totally composed, looking directly into his hooded, flint-toned eyes. She hated his ability to make her feel like she was one of his rumored, high-priced call girls. The man was making her feel totally undressed, and goosebumps prickled up on her tanned skin.

"Ah, yes, Jan. Quite the little iceberg. I'd forgotten."

The brilliant glare assured Jan he'd not forgotten a single instance of her abrupt refusals.

"However"—the steely eyes narrowed dangerously—"one can't help but hear rumors. And the latest one making the rounds is that a certain illustrious newsman is able to melt a little of that ice. Has Dave Barrie been getting into your pants, Jan?"

The crimson rose in a blaze of fury and Jan felt as if she were going to explode.

"That's disgusting! And I'm not going to stand another moment of your filthy accusations." She whirled on a bare heel, reaching for the doorknob.

"One moment, Jan," his sinister voice made her stop. "Just remember one thing. You're in a position of responsibility here at the club. If your relationship with Barrie becomes unsavory, you'll have to be dismissed. We can't have you corrupting the young minds under your care, now, can we? I think, however, that you and I should be able to work out a compromise solution."

There it was. The standard, not-so-veiled threat.

"James ..." Jan turned toward him, favoring

him with a sweet, false smile. Maybe she *would* hold him under until he drowned.

He answered the smile, capped teeth flashing, she decided, like a hungry shark.

"Yes, sweet?" James Waring moved toward her, obviously expecting final capitulation.

"Go to hell!"

Chapter Ten

The door slammed behind Jan with a resounding bang. She went to the showers, crumpling her clothes into a tight bundle.

"Go home," she announced as she marched furiously past the group of openmouthed teenagers. "Practice is over!"

Planning on doing exactly that herself, Jan strode to the parking lot and threw her clothes on the seat beside her. Bare feet stomped on the gas pedal as she twisted the key and sent the car screeching out of the lot with an angry snarl of the engine.

"Damn, damn, damn!" She pounded her fists on the steering wheel. The clicking sound was the last straw, releasing a torrent of hot, angry tears. Something was creating an earsplitting racket on the side of her car. Pulling off the road, she opened the door, checking to see if something had caught in it and was banging against the side. But to Jan's unschooled gaze, everything looked just fine. As soon as she began to drive down the road again, the clattering started once more.

Jan pulled into the dealership where she'd purchased the car, taking her place in the short line to the service department.

"What's the problem, lady?"

The bored service man's eyes brightened visibly

as he looked up from his battered clipboard to view Jan, skimpily clad in the still damp tank suit.

"Something's rattling," she said. "And I'm afraid to drive it home this way."

"Tell you what. You scoot over and we'll take it for a test run and see if we can't locate the problem. Hey, Roy," he hollered over his shoulder, "I'm gonna take this little lady for a spin and see what's wrong. You write up the orders for a few minutes." He flipped the clipboard in the direction of the dark-haired man who'd ambled over.

Jan knew she was being paranoid, but she'd already dodged one unwelcomed pass today. And, she reminded herself, even paranoiacs have enemies. She didn't want to put herself in a position for a second overture. As it was, her nerves were about as frayed as her cut-off jeans. She gathered her clothes to her chest.

"Why don't I just wait inside," she suggested, "while you take it for that test run?"

She was out of the car before he could protest, and Jan heard the grunt of reluctant assent as she headed toward the service department's waiting room.

She held her head high and did her best to ignore the flurry of wolf whistles her appearance caused. The asphalt was hot and it was all she could do to keep her bare feet from skipping as the short walk to the waiting room seemed to take as long as the Bataan Death March.

She'd thrown her clothes over the tank suit by the time the man returned, a disappointed droop tugging at his mouth when he saw her. Still, those bright eyes told her, what was visible under the cut-offs and T-shirt was more than passable.

"Got someone playing tricks on you, lady? Sounds like something's stuck inside the door. Happens sometimes. Guy at the assembly plant's mad at the line foreman. Sticks some bolts or a Coke bottle inside a door well or under the fender. Any number of things possible."

"Well," Jan asked with a polite smile, trying not to show she was running out of patience, "do you think you could check it out?"

"Sure. Take four, maybe five hours."

"Four or five hours? Just to check a little thing like that?"

"Well, sure. There's all those other cars in line ahead of you. You should really have come in before eight this morning, you know," he confided. "If you want the car out today."

"It wasn't rattling at eight this morning," Jan replied through gritted teeth. "Look. I can't wait around here. Let me just give you whatever information you need and I'll pick up the car tomorrow. All right? And could you call me a cab for now?"

He shrugged, pushing back the brim of his yellow San Diego Padres baseball cap. "Sure, lady. Whatever you want."

The necessary paperwork dispensed with, Jan leaned her head back against the sticky vinyl seat of the taxi, taking a deep, soothing breath. What else could possibly go wrong today?

Whatever it was, it wasn't going to be the arrival of Dave Barrie, Jan realized joyously as she opened the door to his brief knock. Her heart leaped in response to the tall, lean man in her doorway, and Dave moved quickly into her living room, drawing her to him, his arms filled with her.

Jan's mouth had been opened with a greeting that was promptly smothered by his warm lips as they covered hers. His breath was hot as those same lips branded her with a searing fire, grazing her cheekbones, her eyelids, her temples, the line of her chin.

"Oh, babe," he growled as he drew her into his

hard body, practically crushing the breath from her lungs, "you feel so damn good to me."

If Dave was desperate for the feel of her, Jan was no less hungry. With a long, shuddering breath she opened her lips to the savage thrusting of his tongue. Her lips closed around it, drawing it into her velvet warmth, and Dave groaned deep in his throat.

"Oh, Jan, I don't want to wait any longer," he said, the anguished words coming out in a harsh rasp, so unlike the controlled modulated tones of the professional newsman. "I guess you win, babe. Because I want you, sweetheart. I need you so much!"

He lowered his tawny head, his warm, mobile lips moving down her throat to nibble on her sensitive collarbone. They continued down the open neck of her blouse, and her skin burned behind the heated path.

When met with the obstacle of material, his hands quickly dispensed with the buttons in an almost-savage craving, pulling them loose to expose her dusky, sun-bronzed breasts. He raised his head momentarily, blue eyes displaying his delight to Jan as he discovered her without the further restriction of a bra. At the smoky, suggestive look, she could feel her nipples gathering themselves into expectant little points.

Dave's tongue traced circles on her yielding flesh, creating an incredible, intense longing in Jan. She thrust her fingers through his hair, pressing him into her softness. When his lips moved and he took the hard, rosy crown between his teeth, she heard a low, inarticulate sound and realized with dazed wonder that it had escaped her own lips.

His hands moved across her hips to her flat stomach, and he lowered the zipper of her silk skirt, letting it slide down her hips in a whisper to the floor. His fingers moved under the satiny material of her half-slip, his hips shifting and moving deliberately as he lifted her thighs into his.

"Dave . . . oh, please, darling."

Jan wanted him to make love to her more than anything she'd ever wanted in her life. She wanted him and she needed him. And she loved him. It was time.

"I love you," she whispered against his marauding lips, clinging to him desperately as if to accentuate her long-awaited declaration.

Dave's eyes seemed to light like fireworks at Jan's admission, the sparks flaring out to both warm and thrill her. His breath was coming in short, hard drafts, and his hands left her just long enough to tug his shirt off and fling it to the floor over her skirt and blouse.

Jan felt the soft mat of his chest hairs brushing against her breasts and gave a muffled groan of impatience as she clung to him, allowing his knee to open her thighs. She needed fulfillment of this shattering urgency and knew that only he could give it to her. Hunger rose and flared in her like a savage spirit, and by the rugged force of his hands as they roamed her arched, willing body, Jan knew her driving needs were echoed in Dave.

His hands created searing sensations as he finished undressing her, never ceasing his erotic caresses. The intimacy of their touching bodies caused Jan to go faint with pleasure and she swayed as he picked her up, his lips hot and ravenous over hers.

Carrying her to her bedroom, Dave placed her down onto the mattress. He stood over her for an agonizingly long moment, his eyes shadowed with unfulfilled passion as they roved the warm curves of her body. His blue gaze feasted on her as he undressed, then he joined her, lying on his side, his long, lean body stretched to its full length. Jan reached for him, attempting to urge his body over hers.

"Uh uh," he murmured, his lips burning kisses all over her. "Not yet. I've been thinking about this for too long to rush it now. I want to make love to you properly."

"I don't know if that's a very winning idea," Jan gasped as his lips skimmed her body from the top of her head down to the sensitive spot at the inside of her ankle. Down her back and along her legs, he moved and bent her to his will. Her dark head tossed on the pillow as Dave proceeded to lead her to the very brink of oblivion.

"You'll see," he murmured against the throbbing fullness of her breasts, "it's one of the best ideas I've ever had. And if you don't like it"—he sucked at the hard nipple and a surge of warmth reached the very depths of her feminine core—"we'll just keep it up until you do."

Dave's hands moved with practiced ravishment over her, fueling Jan's hot, dark tide of passion. His lips moved seductively to follow the trail of his delicate fingertips, his tongue trailing warm, wet fire as it seared into all the sensitive hollows of her awakened flesh.

Jan twisted convulsively, her head thrown back as passion racked her bones. Then in a surge of fiery need that promised to devour her, Dave groaned against her lips, his body meeting her frantic upward thrusts, the thundering of his heart pounding against her breasts.

There was a sudden, golden blaze as he claimed total possession, and only a few strong strokes were needed before they both exploded into a kaleidoscope of brilliance. Jan felt the deep shudder of his body against hers, the long sigh shaking through him, echoing her own trembling.

The blood was still pounding in her ears some time later, and she was content to bask in the warm afterglow of their lovemaking. Jan's senses tingled in response to the soft, tracing fingertip Dave ran down her hip and thigh.

"If that's the way you welcome a fella home," he murmured, his lips against her hair as she rested her head on his chest, "perhaps I should go away more often."

"That's a terrible idea," she whispered. "I was so incredibly lonely without you. The kids think I'm a cross between Genghis Khan and Attila the Hun."

"Not even close." He cast a lazy, provocative eye down her spent, nude body. "Neither of them could've imagined such passion. You ever direct that sexual energy into something else, darlin', and you'll rule the world."

"I don't want the world." *Just you,* she thought. *All I want is this moment—but I want it to last forever.*

"When are you going to marry me?"

Jan's startled eyes circled the room, avoiding the keen blue gaze she knew was studying her reaction.

"Marry?" Her voice couldn't even qualify as a squeak.

"Marry. As in man and wife, woman and husband, you and I."

Jan stared at her hands as she twisted the ginger hairs of his chest, not daring to look him in the eye. She had told the man she loved him, hadn't she? Why couldn't that be enough?

"Oh, Dave . . . it would never work."

"Why not?"

She shook her dark head. "I've been married."

"So? I'm a little old to be expecting a virgin bride. Which, considering the last few minutes, I could hardly request in our case anyway. Not to mention your alleged moments of insanity in

Phoenix." His lips brushed her bare shoulder in a tender gesture. "And I've been married. I didn't realize there was a new California law prohibiting second marriages between consenting adults."

Jan could feel his studied examination, but she didn't feel safe facing him. She knew that her love for him and her aversion to marriage would be warring all across her face, and he'd read them both.

"I can't marry you. I'd make a miserable wife," she murmured softly.

"Why?" Dave demanded. "Because you never have any food in your house? Because you get so wrapped up in your work you'd live on candy bars if I didn't feed you? Because that same work takes you away for days at a time? Because you're not Donna Reed?"

"Partly."

It was a whisper. God, she realized with an earth-shattering knowledge, she loved this man so very, very much. But to play the role of a dutiful little wife would be hell for her. She could pretend happiness for a time, but only a very short time. Her dissatisfaction would soon surface and she'd poison the relationship for them both. No strings. No ties. They'd only end up strangling the enjoyment they'd discovered.

Once you were married, you surrendered your identity. She'd been Jon Elliot's girl-diver-wife and it had taken years to establish a sense of herself after that. She couldn't—wouldn't—let that happen again. Not even for Dave.

Then, although she'd backed away from confronting it, there was that nagging feeling that she didn't really know Dave Barrie. There was far too much of him hiding beneath that easygoing surface. Who would she be agreeing to marry?

"I don't want Donna Reed," he said, his voice strained. "I want you. Just the way you are."

"But—"

He put a finger over her lips. "I grew up in Odessa, Texas," he said in a low voice. "In a mobile home park that would make the neighborhood around El Diablo look like Disneyland."

"Dave, you don't have to—"

"Jan, I do. Would you just listen? And not interrupt at every little thing you find a bit painful? We might never get through this, otherwise."

"All right." Jan nodded, realizing that he was about to strengthen the ties, to bind her irrevocably to him. But she was powerless to refuse. She needed to know.

"My dad spent his life between jobs and between bottles," he said, his tone deathly flat. "While he never managed to find that elusive job, the bottle always seemed to come a great deal easier. Finally one day he did us a favor and took off. I heard a few years later that he'd died in Galveston. I didn't care."

She gasped, and as she risked a glance upward, Jan saw that his eyes had turned to blue glass. Dave's voice was harsh, the usually soft consonants edged with a sharp twang. "I think he did me the biggest favor of all that day he left. I was thirteen and had made the decision that if he hit my mother one more time, I'd kill him. He took off before I had to."

Jan's blood turned ice-cold. Not at the story. She'd heard similar ones in her five years at El Diablo pool. What caused the involuntary shudder was the knowledge that Dave would have done it, that he'd be capable of such a thing. She thanked God for the middle-class, surburban upbringing that had enabled her to never have to discover how hard she could become.

"I got a job on the oil rigs as a roughneck and supported us as well as I could. Finally, when I was eighteen, I knew I had to get out of that town. There was no real future for me. I'd probably end up dead in some knife fight one night, and no one would ever know I'd been alive. Except my mother." His eyes softened. "Believe it or not, you'll like her. She was just born in the wrong place at the wrong time. It took her a while to discover a lady was allowed to think for herself."

Dave smiled and Jan's heart took a tumble. She had to lock her hands together to keep from flinging them around his neck. She wanted to kiss him, to kiss away the reminiscent pain that was shadowing his beautiful blue eyes. But she'd promised not to interrupt.

"I had a girlfriend, of sorts, who wanted to leave Odessa too. Her old man was as violent as mine and she'd spent as many nights hiding out in my place as she did staying home. I didn't see how I could leave her behind. Leave her to that life. So, David Matthew Barrie, eighteen years old, led his womenfolk out of the wilderness to the promised land."

There was a harsh self-mockery in the tone and Jan knew her eyes were brimming with tears. She'd always thought of herself as motivated and strong at eighteen while she'd been working toward her medal. She was surprised Dave didn't find her disgustingly spoiled.

"I joined the navy, which promised a good income and a chance to see more of the world than I'd ever dreamed of while stuck in Texas."

He ran his hands along her shoulders, his eyes holding her moist gaze.

"Listen, Jan. I didn't really want to get married the first time. It just seemed like the right thing to do. So there has never—*never*—been a woman I seriously considered spending my life with. I like

women. I enjoy their company. But marriage—
well, that's always been something for the other
guy. Until you. And I'm old enough to know I'm not
going to meet another woman who affects me the
way you do!"

Jan watched the muscles tensing along his jaw as
he fought for control, reflecting an explosive energy
hidden directly below the surface.

"I don't want you to change, darlin'. Because I'm
not attracted to your housekeeping—or your cook-
ing. And I sure as hell can't be flattered by your
interest in my so-called fame, because you didn't
know me from Adam. I want to marry you because
you're a strong, independent woman. You're constantly striving for that extra something that puts
you above the others. I admire that. And I realize it
will keep me from receiving your full, undivided,
adoring attention.

"But you excite me, babe. And I love you. I've
been trying to take things slowly so you'd have to
admit we had more going for us than a strong sexual attraction. But I want to start spending my life
with you. I want you lying in my arms. All night.
Every night we can, forever."

Jan's eyes finally overflowed, tears running down
her cheeks as she fell into his arms. "I do love you,
Dave . . . but please, give me a little more time."

"It's not the answer I wanted, darlin'," he murmured, burying his lips in the pulse spot at the base
of her neck, "but I can't deny you anything your
sweet little heart desires." His voice was a deep,
lazy drawl. "You've got your extension. Just don't
keep me in suspense too long?"

"Not long," she agreed. While she couldn't
immediately accept his proposal, there were other
things Jan could do to demonstrate her love. The
even tenor of Dave's breathing became a ragged
cadence as her fingers danced over him, recalling

his body's needs and desires. She exalted in the knowledge that she could give this beautiful man such pleasure, and when he groaned her name in enraptured bliss, a tremor of expectation shivered through her.

Her lips moved to follow the trail her fingers had blazed, bringing him to the heights he'd led her to earlier. As his ardor grew, so did Jan's, and when Dave pulled her to him, rolling over to cover her with his fiery warmth, she met him with a fervent, blazing hunger.

A flurry of emotion swept through her body like a convulsion and the world tilted, only to right itself again as they shared in the sweet culmination of passion.

Later, lying in his arms, Jan watched the moonlight streaming through the window, accentuating the strong features of this man she loved. Her finger ran down his nose, and she felt a tingling of icy fear as she traversed the crooked bridge, knowing for certain now that it had been broken. But she didn't want to ponder the possibilities as to how, not after the story he'd told her.

"I'd planned to tell you as soon as I'd kissed you hello," his deep voice broke the golden silence they'd been sharing, "but I got sidetracked."

"Tell me what?" Jan murmured, her lips exploring playful little paths across the warm, moist skin of his chest. She found the dark nipple hidden in the red-gold carpeting of soft hair and circled her teeth around it, plucking gently.

"Stop it." He laughed, pulling her head up by her glossy dark hair. "We'll never get this conversation over with."

"All right." Jan heaved a huge sigh, returning her head to his shoulder, where she couldn't help but scatter a few kisses against his neck. It was as if

she couldn't get enough of the feel and taste of Dave
Barrie, she loved him so very, very much.

"I've made a decision. I'm taking the cable job."

Jan's green eyes flew from the earlobe she'd been
nibbling to his face, searching intently. "Really?"

Dave drew her closer, fitting her curves to his
body. "Really."

"And what you told me about location . . . ?"

"Right. They're willing to let me anchor here. I'll
still have to do some traveling, but nothing like I've
been doing. Probably a good thing, really. My
absences will keep you from getting bored with
me."

Jan played with the tousled ginger hair skim-
ming his forehead. "Bored? Never. Not in a billion
years. But the network—" She clamped her mouth
shut, her teeth making a sound that reverberated in
her ears. Why in the world was she citing the network's case? They had enough people of their own
that were paid to do that. This was the time to shut
her mouth and count her blessings.

"Has been very good to me," he finished. "But it
hasn't been one-sided. I've been good to them, too.
And if I took them up on their offer, as sure as there
are ratings, they'd plunk me down on the air opposite some sophomoric situation comedy on another
network. Suddenly my entire career would depend
on whether or not a test group of viewers got sweaty
palms when they watched me. I don't want my
life's work to come down to whether or not I turn
people on."

"I can't imagine you not," Jan answered truthfully, snuggling against him.

Dave dropped a light kiss against her head. "Ah,
but you've already managed to convince me you're
crazy."

"Crazy about you," Jan whispered, covering his
lips with her own for a long, delightful kiss.

"Now that we've got my career all settled," Dave said as they reluctantly came up for air, "how about yours? What have you told Bob?"

"I haven't decided. A lot's been happening."

Jan told him everything, glossing lightly over her encounter with James Waring. At least she thought she'd glossed over it; the fire in his blue eyes told her differently.

"That bastard's asking to get himself drowned in his own pool," Dave growled savagely.

Jan was stunned and frightened by his stinging, ruthless tone. It occurred to her that the only time those smooth, modulated deep tones betrayed Dave's Texas origin was when he was making love to her, or reverting to more treacherous methods to win something he wanted. At those times the polished facade would slip a bit, giving a glimpse of a highly passionate man.

While the drawl had returned, it was not the soft, soothing tone he used when making love. It now had the harshness of a bullwhip. His tanned face had turned pewter gray with tension, and Jan reached up, running her fingers lightly over the tightly bunched muscles of his jaw.

"Hey," she murmured, "I'm a big girl. I can take care of myself."

"Rotten bastard. If he ever so much as looks at you again, I'll kill him!"

Something she'd never experienced firsthand from Dave blazed in his crystal eyes, and Jan shuddered from the apprehension that feathered its way up her bare spine in response.

"Dave, darling. Please. Let's just forget it."

The stormy light of battle eventually dimmed as his eyes shifted, moving across her desperate face. His silent appraisal seemed to go on forever, and then the look softened, his drawn lips relaxing into a humorless line of resignation.

"I know," Dave muttered. "I promised you I'd let you lead your own life. But there are certain things women have, by nature, a disadvantage at. And creeps like Waring know it."

"I've been dodging his kind for years."

"If you married me, Jan, you wouldn't have to."

"That's no reason to get married, Dave, for some type of protection. Besides, I don't think it would make much difference." Jan gave him a little smile, making a weak attempt at levity. "A Doberman pinscher would probably be more effective."

"Marriage would," Dave argued, his firm jaw jutting out. "Because anyone who dared to try anything with my wife would be notified that their days were numbered the minute they were stupid enough to make one move toward you."

He groaned, rubbing his hand over his face before raking the long fingers through his hair. "Listen to me. I sound like a goddamn Neanderthal. And here I am, trying to convince you I wouldn't be an overbearing husband."

"Let's not talk about it tonight," Jan suggested softly. "I'm just glad to have you home."

Dave pulled her back to him, his fingers splayed against the small of her back.

"Me too, babe. Me too."

Jan barely heard the doorbell the next morning. Dave was in the shower and the pelting drone of the water plus the lusty male tones raised in song, muffled the chimes.

"Damn."

She'd been debating joining him. Sighing, she got out of bed to slip on a terry robe. She was on her way to answer the insistent ringing when Dave emerged from the bathroom, his voice muffled from the folds of the towel he had over his head as he rubbed his hair dry.

"You expecting someone?"

"No. I can't imagine who it is."

Jan allowed herself the unmitigated pleasure of viewing his tall, hard body clad only in a brief, sunshine-yellow towel before she left the room. Whoever it was obviously meant to keep his finger on the button until she opened the door.

"Yes?" Jan's fingers plucked at the edges of her robe, drawing them together as she peered around the door at the two gray-suited men standing on her front porch.

"Ms. Baxter? Jan Baxter?" The taller of the men addressed her politely, but with a stiff formality.

"Yes." She nodded slowly, beginning to experience an odd feeling of fear. "I'm Jan Baxter."

"I'm Sergeant Jamison, Ms. Baxter. And this is Sergeant Shaw. We're with the police department."

He flipped open a case the size of Jan's credit-card holder, letting her see the official-looking identification card and shield. "Did you leave your car at Monte Vista Auto yesterday?"

Her eyes widened. "Why, yes. Was it stolen?"

Jan had heard of that. Car-theft rings operating inside car dealerships. Her heart sank at the thought of losing her beautiful car. The insurance would replace it, but it had been the first car she'd ever specially ordered. She'd met Dave in that car. She loved it.

"No, ma'am. It's fine." He looked over his shoulder, appearing uncomfortable. "Would you mind discussing this inside?"

Jan felt the prickle of fear grow stronger at his coolly polite request. "Of course. Just a moment," she replied, schooling her voice to a calm she certainly didn't feel. She shut the door momentarily to slip the chain from its track and reopened it, gesturing the two men inside.

"Would you care for coffee?" she asked, her smile feeling as frozen as Howdy Doody's wooden grin. "It'll only take a moment."

"No, thank you." The second man only shook his head negatively. "Ms. Baxter, after you left your car yesterday, a bottle of illegal drugs was discovered inside the left front-door panel. Would you have any idea as to the origin of those drugs?"

Drugs! Jan felt her knees buckle under her and she reached blindly for the nearest thing to hold on to. It was the arm of a white wicker chair and she lowered herself shakily into it.

Chapter Eleven

❧

"Is Ms. Baxter a suspect?" The sound of Dave's voice had Jan turning toward him with a flood of heartfelt relief.

If Jan was surprised to see Dave enter the room, droplets of water still sparkling in his hair from the shower, it was nothing compared to the surprise etched on the faces of the two men. She noticed at once an easing of their hard, formal stance.

"No, sir. It stands to reason, since it was the container of pills making the noise in her car, that Ms. Baxter never would have taken it into the shop if she'd been involved. We'd just like her cooperation to determine where she may have been when those drugs were stashed."

His attention returned to Jan, but this time the Sergeant's eyes didn't seem to pierce her with quite the same professional intensity. "You teach at El Diablo pool, don't you?"

"Yes, but—"

"We'd like you to come downtown and give us a statement. It's possible that one of your students down there has been using you as a courier."

Jan's ashen cheeks regained some of their color as twin flags of scarlet reflected her anger. "Sergeant, if there's one thing I'm sure of, it's that none of those kids would do that to me. I've spent five years building a relationship of trust with them. And that trust works both ways!"

"You wouldn't be the first bleeding heart to get burned."

Boy, Jan thought, glaring at Sergeant Shaw, when the guy decided to open his mouth, he could be a real sweetie!

"I'm sure you know the statistics far better than I, Sergeant." Her voice was as brisk as a February day in Buffalo. "But I know those kids. Besides, the noise wasn't there yesterday when I drove to work. Only when I left. And La Conquista is located in La Jolla. Which, you'll have to agree, is a major distance, not only socially, but geographically, from El Diablo."

"We just need a statement, Ms. Baxter," Sergeant Jamison stepped in to regain control of the conversation. "It won't take long."

Jan looked over at Dave, her green eyes distressed, silently asking him what to do. At this moment, she wasn't even sure she could stand. She'd take all the help she could get.

"I'll bring Ms. Baxter down to the station as soon as she's dressed," he announced.

Jan threw him a wobbly, grateful smile.

"We're prepared to take her with us, sir."

"Sergeant." Dave gave him a friendly, disarming grin, the tone in his voice firmer than the smile would indicate. "I assure you, I've no intention of taking Ms. Baxter and making a run for the border. I'll personally deliver her to the station within the hour. I'm sure that will satisfy Captain Donaldson."

There it was again. So faint that anyone not paying strict attention to his voice might have missed it. That drawl. It was only an implied threat, and so veiled that it was obvious neither detective knew if it had even been one, but the mention of their superior's name did the trick and they both turned toward the door.

"That will be fine, Mr. Barrie," Sergeant Jamison said stiffly. "Thank you for your assistance."

"No problem. I'm glad to be able to help."

Dave walked them to the door, seeing them out as if it was his house. Jan hadn't moved from the chair. In fact, she thought as she gripped the wicker arms and her nails dug into the soft wood, she wasn't even certain she could. She'd never even had a parking ticket before. The thought of making some official statement to the police made her feel sick.

She knew she looked as bad as she felt when Dave returned to stand over her, his keen eyes dark with compassion.

"It'll be fine, honey," he said softly. "Here, put your head between your knees." He squatted down beside her, coaxing her dark head to a lowered position in an attempt to bring some blood back to her brain.

But suddenly Jan's stomach gave an incredible flop, worse than a triple somersault with a half-gainer, and she lurched out of the chair, stumbling toward the bathroom.

"Here." Dave ran the water in the sink, wetting a washcloth, which he used to gently wash her face. "Better?"

"I think so." Jan was sitting on the bathroom floor, her head resting back against the blue-and-white-tiled wall.

Dave stepped over her, reaching to turn on the shower. "Can you do this by yourself? Want some help?" He gave her an intimate smile, and Jan noted with a rush of love that there wasn't the least suggestion of sexual provocation to his question. His blue eyes were deep pools of concern.

"I'll be O.K. Really," she added as she saw the flicker of doubt cross his unguarded eyes.

He left her then, and as Jan ran the soap over the body he'd claimed as his own, she thought how lucky she was to have Dave at her side right now. She wondered about her insistence for total autonomy. She certainly hadn't rushed in to stop his smooth interference earlier!

"You look beautiful!" Dave offered as she entered the kitchen. "You'll have an entire precinct falling head over heels in love with you."

The thin pinstripes on the white background of the crisp cotton sundress were buttercup yellow, the sleeveless style dipping to a modest V in back. It was a dress that managed to create an aura of cool comfort on the hottest day, and it was now giving Jan a look of composure. One she was far from feeling.

"Here." He offered her a piece of fragrant cinnamon toast. "Eat this in the car. It'll help settle your stomach."

"Thank you. For everything." A horrible thought had occurred to Jan in the shower and she had to share it with Dave. She took a deep breath for courage.

"Dave?"

"Yeah, babe?"

"A long time ago—before the Olympics—I had a little problem, uh, with some medication. You don't think that they'll . . ." Her voice drifted off on a choked sob.

"Think you're giving drugs to your divers just because when you were eighteen Elliot made a mistake and let your doctor change your asthma medication? Don't be silly, babe. You're looking for trouble that just doesn't exist."

"You knew?"

"I knew. And all I'm going to say about the entire

stupid mistake is that you survived the mess like the champ you are. Just like we're going to get through today."

She put her arms about his waist, resting her head against his shoulder for a long moment, as if to gather her strength. "Do you have any idea how good you are for me?" she whispered.

"Of course I do, darlin'. I just didn't know how long it'd take you to realize it."

Dave reached down and placed his fingers under her lowered chin, raising it so he could look into her eyes. That magic smile lit his face before his curved lips covered hers in a brief, reassuring kiss.

"Come on, darlin'," he murmured, his jaw against Jan's hair as he stroked it comfortingly. "Let's get this foolishness over with so we can get on with our reunion. I'm all in favor of being a good citizen, but when it cuts into my love life, I begin to lose patience."

"How did it go?"

"Fine," Jan told Dave as she came out of the room that had held only herself, a police stenographer, and a nice, friendly officer who'd reminded her of her father. "He was really quite nice."

"No rubber hoses?" There was a hint of a smile at the corner of his mouth.

"Nope. Not a one." Jan took the hand he'd extended and allowed hers to snuggle into it as Dave led her down the maze of hallways. It was the same way they'd come in, but earlier the building had just seemed like an olive-green blur to Jan. Turning a corner, she was surprised to see James Waring approaching them. She didn't like the pressure she felt being applied to her fingers as Dave spotted him, too.

"Jan." He blocked their way, a foolish thing to

do, she thought. Jan flinched at Dave's crushing grip on her hand, but he didn't seem to notice.

"Yes?"

"I had a call from a local television station, asking for my reaction to the unsavory news that you were down here concerning illegal drugs hidden in your car. Do you have any idea what this has done for my day?"

"Probably about the same thing it did for mine," Jan answered, trying to move around him. She didn't like the man, but the tension radiating from Dave was even more disconcerting. "Not exactly peachy, is it?"

The man's a fool, she decided as he continued to block her exit.

"Jan, I've spoken to you before about this flippant attitude concerning the example you're setting for our young people. I must warn you—"

"Just one bloody moment here." Dave's deep voice rumbled like thunder and Jan stepped back instinctively as he released his iron grip on her hand. The drawl was back, a harsh weapon in itself.

"Look here, Waring. I've been informed of your slimy advances toward Ms. Baxter and I can't see where you're in any position to speak of examples."

Dave moved forward as he spoke, backing James Waring against the drab olive wall of the deserted hallway. A long finger made stabbing motions at the smaller man's chest. Dave didn't touch him, Jan noted, but he conveyed the overt threat of bodily harm just the same.

Dave was glaring down like an angry Titan. "For the record, if you so much as look in her direction again, you'll find your office filled with television cameras while I do an in-depth probe into sexual harassment in the workplace. Is that understood?"

"You wouldn't dare. That would be blatant, prejudicial, yellow journalism."

Jan had to give the little worm credit. He was still struggling to maintain that image of suave urbanity.

"You damn well bet it would," Dave growled. "You see, Waring, I'm extremely prejudiced where this woman is concerned. And I promise you that any harm that comes to her would require me to ensure the total destruction of the man who caused it."

The drawl thickened and Dave Barrie could have been back in the oilfields. "You might consider it a vendetta. There wouldn't be a move you'd make that I wouldn't be watching. Pretty soon, you'd run out of rocks to hide under. And you'd be doing it on network television. Give it some thought."

Dave spun on his heel, put his arm about Jan's waist, and practically lifted her off the floor as he pulled her down the hallway.

"Hey! Wait a minute," she gasped, running to keep up with his long, angry strides.

Dave slowed immediately at the desperation in her voice and the harsh fury dissolved from his features.

"I'm sorry, babe. I just had to get out of there. I was going to put that little jerk's face through the nearest wall."

Jan's eyes were huge green circles as she fought to catch her breath. "Remember when I accused you of being ruthless?"

"I remember. I don't think I denied it."

"You're scary when you get wound up."

"Don't ever be misled by the easygoing exterior, Jan," he warned, suddenly serious. "Just because I've learned to polish up the rough edges doesn't mean I'm a pushover."

"I realize that."

His eyes held hers and Jan was vitally aware of the power surging through him. Then suddenly he gave her a broad, deliberate wink, and the relief washed over her in cool waves.

"Come on," Dave said, his hand snaking about her waist. "We still haven't had breakfast, and I'd definitely planned to serve up something special."

"Breakfast in bed?" Jan smiled.

"Smart girl."

As they left the darkened interior of the police station, they were hit simultaneously by the glare of the sun and the unexpected questions from the press who were camped all over the steps.

"Mr. Barrie! Dave!" One particularly strident female voice rang out over the other shouted queries. "Are you here with Ms. Baxter because of your probe on drugs in youth sports?"

Dave's face hardened to sculpted granite as he watched Jan pale. "No comment," he growled, shoving her into the front seat of his car before fighting his way through the pressing crowd of his fellow reporters to make his way to the driver's side.

"Don't say a word," he warned her as he twisted the key and pulled the car out of the parking lot, scattering the dodging reporters. "Not one single word right now."

Jan slumped in the seat, overcome by the events of the morning. She glanced down at her watch. It was only ten o'clock. How in the world could so many things have gone wrong so early in the day?

The heavy silence ricocheted around the car's interior as neither of them spoke. Dave's attention was glued to the roadway ahead as he drove the car out of the city. Jan was afraid to ask him where they were going, but soon she recognized the road leading to the Torrey Pines State Park.

The only sound was the occasional screech of tires as he threw the car around the curves, climbing the bluffs between Del Mar and La Jolla. The trees protected in the confines were some of the rarest in the world, appearing only in San Diego and a small island off the coast of Santa Barbara. Rangers regularly escorted guests on walks through the park, explaining the delicate ecosystems of the San Diego region. But Jan knew Dave wasn't heading toward the beautiful park for a guided tour.

He suddenly pulled the car off the road, scattering gravel beneath the wheels. Turning to him, Jan was surprised to see that the look in his eyes wasn't anger, as she'd suspected, but a deep, defensive shadow.

"All right, we'd better get this out in the open. You're still having problems with it, aren't you? The fact that I showed up poolside and forged my way into your life at the same time I happened to be working on that sports probe." His mouth tightened at the response in her eyes. Jan couldn't deny it.

"And since you've accused me of being a ruthless individual when I'm after something I want, you can't help wondering if all this attention I've lavished on you is nothing but a covert plot to gain an inside track. Especially since drugs have shown up at La Conquista. Right?"

Dave looked for a fleeting second as if Jan had stabbed him with a sharp spear as she nodded slowly, honestly, in the affirmative.

She jumped as a hand reached out past her, but Dave was only opening her door. "I want you to take some time to think about everything," he said. "I'm not taking you home right away because your house will be surrounded by reporters. And by now my apartment will be, too. So you'll have to do your thinking alone out here. When you're ready to talk, I'll be waiting."

He understood so much, Jan thought. She did need to be alone right now. She had to sort everything out. She walked along a narrow pathway, feeling his eyes on her back until she took a sharp turn and was out of his sight. The yellow daisies flanked the seaward sides of the bluffs, the moisture from the sea sustaining a deep-green, scattered growth. The small, twisted pines blanketed the steep bluffs and Jan walked to the edge, gazing down at the foam-laced surf as it pounded against the rocks far below. The rugged water had carved out secluded beaches and she watched the careful movements of a lone beachcomber as he walked along the packed, wet sand.

It was a peaceful, quiet place, perfect for introspection. As usual, Dave had been right. He always seemed to know everything she was feeling. Always one step ahead of her.

Could he have been using her as an inside source? Was the Dave Barrie who'd survived the oil fields of Odessa, Texas, ruthless enough to do such a thing? He'd admitted his desire to kill his own father, if necessary. And she'd been terrified during the confrontation with James Waring. Could he have been so willing to hurt her? For a story?

Jan reviewed their time together, every minute, from that first day she'd broken all her rules and picked up a strange man on a deserted highway to the present. When she'd reached this morning, Jan turned back to the car.

Dave was leaning against the front fender in much the same way he'd been standing that first moment she'd laid eyes on him. Leaning against the car, long legs crossed in front of him, arms folded across his chest, his tawny head lifted as she approached, but he didn't make a move toward her.

They stood there, a span of a few feet separating them, but it seemed to be a gaping chasm as wide and as deep as the Grand Canyon. Jan's sandaled foot traced patterns in the dust as she considered her next move. Dave remained very still, awaiting her reaction.

She narrowed the gap between them, standing a hairs breadth from him as she looked up into his stony face. A face she loved, but barely recognized right now.

"You really do love me," she said softly.

All the tension seemed to flow from his body and his eyes took on a strange expression. "Of course I do."

"I wasn't certain. Until just a few minutes ago."

His steady blue eyes looked at her with gentle censure. "You should have been. I've known from the beginning. But what made you realize it now?"

Jan knew she'd die if he didn't take her in his arms, but Dave seemed willing to wait until the necessary words had been dispensed with. Every pore, every nerve in her body was tuned to whatever frequency he was operating on, and she reached out to take his strong wrists, her thumbs tracing patterns on the warm skin at the inside of them.

"You misused your position and power. Or threatened to, with James."

"I'd do everything I said." His voice was harsh, the polish sliding away once again to reveal the angry drawl. Jan's eyes were brimming with her love as she looked up into the renewed fury that flashed in his face at the memory.

"I know. And it would have been a foolish thing to do. You're not careless where your work is concerned. Only people in love are that dumb." She smiled, a warm caress. "And you're going to show up on every television screen in the country tonight, attempting to run down a group of your colleagues as you're leaving the police station with your lover. A woman discovered to have an cache of illegal drugs in her car."

"They were harassing you. I couldn't allow that."

"They were doing their jobs," Jan argued softly, a trace of humor reasserting itself in her voice. "As you've done, a million times, yourself. But it was suddenly different."

"Of course. You're different."

Jan's hands moved from his wrists, up his arms to encircle his neck. "And that's how I knew," she murmured, drawing his head down for a kiss she'd been wanting for far too long already.

His lips molded her mouth in an all-consuming flare of passion and Jan was swept with a sudden weakness as the kiss made her adrenaline surge. She was pliant in his arms and had to lean against him for support.

"Let's go home, babe," Dave breathed into her ear.

Jan nodded, not caring what might greet her when she arrived. She only wanted to be home with him, where she knew she'd be safe.

The phone was ringing as they entered, and Dave held her back, preventing her from answering it. "It's probably just a reporter. Let it ring."

"I'd better answer it. By now my folks have probably heard the news and I'd hate to have them worry." She extricated herself from Dave's embrace.

When Jan returned from the kitchen, she had a deep furrow on her forehead and her eyes were glittering with a moist sheen.

"Jan?" Dave was by her side in two swift strides, gathering her into the cocoon of his arms. "What's the matter?"

"That call was from Phoenix. From the Cassidys. It seems that Jon assured them he'd be glad to take over Jimmy's training if they were uncomfortable with my unsavory reputation. How could he do something like that?"

Her face twisted with shock and anger, and Dave kissed away the tears that trickled down her cheeks. This was the last straw, she thought furiously.

"He's a creep," Dave said, "always was. Just because you were married to the guy doesn't mean the toad automatically turned into a prince." He gave her a boisterous grin. "You have to find those of us who are just naturally princes to begin with. Forget the toad," he coaxed, his hands moving suggestively at the base of her spine.

Jan was still fuming about the injustice of it as Dave led her into the bedroom, undressing her determinedly. He pulled back the covers on the still-unmade bed.

"Take a little rest, sweetheart," he advised. "You've earned it."

"Alone?" Her green eyes invited him to bed. Jan couldn't think of anything that would make her feel better, make her forget this miserable morning, than to have Dave to join her.

His lips twitched. "Alone." He nodded, his eyes smiling. "I've got a few calls to make."

She heard the dialing of the phone and his low drone before she fell asleep, emotional exhaustion overcoming her curiosity.

Chapter Twelve

❦

Although Dave caught it on the first ring, the shrill bell on the table next to her head woke Jan up from a light, restless sleep. He was putting the receiver back on its wall hanger as she entered the kitchen.

"Who was that?"

"Just a friend. Did you have a good sleep?"

"Restless," Jan admitted. "What friend?"

"It's not important." His face wasn't unfriendly, but it was definitely shuttered. What was he keeping from her?

"Oh, Dave, was it a crank call? Am I getting those now?"

His expression softened as he reached out to massage her shoulders. "No, this was a friend of mine." He let go of her, moving away. "I've got to leave for a while, Jan. Will you be all right?"

"Where are you going?"

"Out."

"Is this about the drugs?" She studied his inscrutable features carefully.

"Jan—" Dave hesitated.

"I remember someone who once stated that he split all the decisions down the middle," she reminded him lightly, but with an obvious note of seriousness. "So what's happening?"

"This doesn't concern you, Jan."

"The hell it doesn't, Dave Barrie! It's all about me. It's *my* car, *my* career, and *I* was the one invited down to the police station this morning. And it's my front yard those damn reporters have been picnicking on. Have you ever seen so many hamburger sacks in one place?"

"They've all gone," he announced.

Jan's eyes widened. "Why? Did they find out who—"

"An anonymous tip." He grinned, his blue eyes dancing with unrestrained glee. "Funny how when one reporter takes off in a direction, the rest follow like a herd of sheep running off a cliff."

Her hand flew to her mouth, stifling the giggle that bubbled forth. "Dave Barrie! You didn't."

"I said anonymous." He grinned. "Now, I do have to go."

"I'm coming with you. Just give me two minutes to throw some clothes on."

"Jan, you can't. It might be dangerous."

"Down the middle," she reminded him over her shoulder. "You'd better wait, mister, or it'll be the last great idea we ever share."

"How long do we wait?" Jan whispered, curled up in the front seat of his car. They'd been parked in an alley on the city's south side for about two hours. It had grown dark and she was becoming visibly nervous.

They'd spent the day driving around to different phone booths. Jan had waited each time while Dave placed the calls. Once, she'd hunched low in her seat as he'd disappeared into a tavern, seemingly unperturbed by the ominous group of motorcycles parked out front. She'd seen parts of San Diego today that she'd never run across in her thirty years of living in the city. And she'd breathed a sigh of relief when he'd emerged from the bar, unscathed, all in one piece, and she'd thought she'd be willing to go another thirty years without reliving the experience.

"Not long," he murmured now, his eyes moving to the rearview mirror. "In fact, I think we've just hit the jackpot."

Jan turned around, peeking over the top of the seat. Her stomach plummeted as she saw the silent caravan entering the alley with their headlights cut.

"Oh, no," she gasped, grabbing his arm. "Dave, there's too many. You'll be killed if you go out there!" Her wild gaze swept around, trying to count the low-riders filling the alley.

"You *are* an innocent." He chuckled, kissing her on the lips lightly. "You can't even tell the good guys from the bad guys without the hats. This, my dear, is the cavalry. Wait here for me."

He left her and walked toward the lead car, hands held loosely to his sides. Jan was more than willing to remain in the car, deciding that not all decisions had to be split precisely down the middle. She did, however, pull a nail file from her purse. It wasn't much. But if anyone laid one finger on Dave Barrie . . .

She knew she was seeing things as Mario emerged from the metallic burgundy low-rider, shaking hands with Dave in a sequence of gestures that Jan would never have been able to duplicate. The two walked a bit away from the others, their heads together, talking quietly in the still night.

After a time, Jan saw Dave dig down into his pocket. As if on cue, two car doors opened swiftly. She held her breath, but nothing happened as he only appeared to be extending some folded bills toward Mario. The young man shook his head firmly and turned to walk away. He climbed back into the low-slung car and led the silent, dark procession past her, exiting the alley.

"I didn't know you knew Mario!" Her expression was one of incredulity as Dave folded his tall frame back into the front seat of his small car.

"I didn't. Not until today."

"But you looked like old friends."

"We're *compadres*," he said simply. "We understand each other. And we both have special feelings for a certain independent, obsessive lady."

Jan shook her head, knowing how hard Mario was to get to know. He didn't trust easily, that one. That he'd accepted Dave so quickly . . .

"I see." She studied him. "You can take the boy off the streets—"

"But you can't take the streets out of the boy," Dave finished for her. She watched as his hands tightened on the steering wheel, and the eyes scanning her face held a certain wary intensity.

"Does it matter?" he asked seriously. "That I'm not all my television image shows me to be?"

"Of course it matters."

"Oh." Dave turned back to look out the windshield, his profile looking as if it had been hewn from marble.

"It matters because it's a part of you. I love the entire man, Dave, not just a smooth, carefully constructed television personality."

Jan leaned in front of him to gain his attention, holding his face between her palms as she placed a series of gentle kisses on his lips, beginning at the corners and working inward.

"I doubt if Dave Barrie, supernewsman, takes ladies for rides on merry-go-rounds, either. And I adore that man. He taught me how to have fun. How to let the child I'd never been to come out and play. But the man who's in this alley right now—

the one from the hard times—he's the one who taught me about commitment."

Jan was caught up in an embrace so tight, so suffocating, that for a fleeting instant she worried that Dave had forgotten how strong he could be. Just when she thought her ribs were in danger of being cracked, he loosened his hold and covered her lips with a long, shuddering kiss.

"God, I love you," he growled, his fingers tangling in her hair.

"And I love you," she whispered.

"Damn," he groaned, putting her back onto her own seat, "we've got to finish this up. Although I can think of several things I'd rather be doing right now. And every one of them is with you."

Jan smiled, warmed by his words. "I've never tried it, but I'd imagine if you want to make love in a car, Dave, we should use mine. I think we're both too tall to make love in the front seat of this sporty BMW you're so fond of."

"You were right," he agreed, pulling the car out of the alley."

"When?"

"That first day. This *is* a stupid car. Next time I'll buy a van."

Dave drove to the deserted parking lot of a shopping mall, parking on the outskirts and cutting the engine and the lights. Then he pulled her over against him, his arm around her so they slumped down in the seat.

Jan didn't know what they were waiting for now, but wrapped safely in his arms, she knew how much she loved this man. And how much she wanted to be all his. Although she'd been willing to let Dave handle this mess, it was because he was the one who was most qualified. What did she know about street crime and drugs? It was a rare occasion when Jan Baxter would even take an aspirin.

No, she wasn't letting him run her life. And he wasn't trying to. He was just helping her, as she'd try to help him if he needed it. They were a team, now, and that's what mattered.

Suddenly the parking lot was ablaze with lights and Jan blinked with the shock and the daytime brightness.

"Be right back," Dave promised, kissing her on the lips with a reassuring hardness.

She watched as he strode across the lot, talking with one of the many policemen who'd suddenly appeared from nowhere. Her mouth dropped open as she watched the young man being put into the back seat of a black-and-white patrol car.

"Was that who I think it was?" she asked as Dave returned.

He nodded, restarting the car and heading home. "James Waring the Fourth," he confirmed dryly.

Jan lapsed into stunned silence. When she was an old woman and had experienced far more of the world than she had now, she knew this would still go down as one of the weirdest days of her life!

"I like this place," Dave said as he put his feet up on the white wicker hassock and leaned back to let his eyes roam over the carvings along the high ceilings of her house. "It's homey. You've made it perfect."

"I'm glad you like it." Jan smiled, sitting on the soft green carpeting, her head resting against his leg. "I'd like to stay here after we're married. Unless you've other plans?"

It didn't even irritate her that Dave wasn't at all surprised when she spoke of her intention to marry him for the first time.

"What plans would I have? I'll be evicted the minute I inform the network about my decision to leave. And after my little display of intemperate behavior this morning, there's a good chance I'll return to find my clothes in a pile outside the door of that sterile penthouse apartment. I'm a homeless waif, kiddo. You'll be performing an act of charity to take me in."

Jan smiled up at him, her heart feeling so full of love that it reminded her of a helium-filled balloon, able to drift right up into the heavens.

"How did you know?"

"About Waring? I didn't really. But it stood to reason it was someone from the club. And you've got such workaholic habits, who'd ever expect you to leave early? If his old man hadn't forced you to run off like you did yesterday, they probably could've gotten away with it."

"But there's twenty-five kids at La Conquista. How did you pinpoint James that fast?"

"I told you, hon. There was already a pretty good trail. And don't forget Mario and his Los Cholos Locos. They were the ones who set up the sale that nailed him. We figured that with his stuff being confiscated, James would have some pretty unhappy customers on his back. We'd hoped he'd be a little careless in his desperation."

"James Waring," she sighed. "And to think his father was threatening me. What kind of example has he been? Let me tell you—"

She was just getting wound up when Dave's head swooped down, smothering her outraged monologue. The bruising force of the kiss silenced her, and Jan was overcome with a rising, elemental need. She opened her lips willingly.

"That's better," his low, vibrating voice murmured against the corner of her mouth. Dave took her hand and led her to the bedroom.

"Dave?"

He took the receiver off the bedroom phone and placed it into a drawer. "Hmm?"

"I'm going to take the job with Bob and the recreation department."

His lips were nibbling at her ear, the warm moisture turning her legs to melted butter. "I knew that."

"How? I just decided," Jan said, her voice choked with emotion as he began to slowly undress her. His lips moved to brush fiery sparks on each part of her newly exposed skin.

"Because those kids need you more. You'll always go where you're most needed." His speech was slurred by desire, his drawl warm and wonderful as his mouth bit into the soft skin of her stomach. "Except now," the muffled tone complained. "I need you more than I can say, and you just keep on talking."

"I wanted you to know."

His hands moved up the insides of her thighs, his caressing, probing fingers drawing a moan of ecstasy from her.

"I knew." Dave grinned rakishly and his clothes joined hers on the floor. He pulled her down on the bed, and his blue eyes gleamed with a glint of pleasant lust. "Now, do you think you can turn your attention to your husband-to-be for a while?"

"For a while," she confirmed, kissing his firm jaw. "A very long while." Her lips reached up and kissed the thin white scar that ran across the bridge of his nose. "A lifetime," she promised.

TELL US YOUR OPINIONS AND RECEIVE A FREE COPY OF THE RAPTURE NEWSLETTER.

Thank you for filling out our questionnaire. Your response to the following questions will help us to bring you more and better books. In appreciation of your help we will send you a free copy of the Rapture Newsletter.

1. Book Title:_____

   Book # :_____ (5-7)

2. Using the scale below how would you rate this book on the following features? Please write in one rating from 0-10 for each feature in the spaces provided. Ignore bracketed numbers.

(Poor) 0 1 2 3 4 5 6 7 8 9 10 (Excellent)
                                             0-10 Rating

Overall Opinion of Book. . . . . _____ (8)
Plot/Story. . . . . _____ (9)
Setting/Location. . . . . _____ (10)
Writing Style. . . . . _____ (11)
Dialogue. . . . . _____ (12)
Love Scenes. . . . . _____ (13)
Character Development:
Heroine:. . . . . _____ (14)
Hero:. . . . . _____ (15)
Romantic Scene on Front Cover. . . . . _____ (16)
Back Cover Story Outline . . . . _____ (17)
First Page Excerpts. . . . . _____ (18)

3. What is your: Education: Age:_____(20-22)

   High School (   )1   4 Yrs. College (   )3
   2 Yrs. College (   )2   Post Grad   (   )4 (23)

4. Print Name:_____

   Address:_____

   City:_____State:_____Zip:_____

   Phone # (   ) _____ (25)

Thank you for your time and effort. Please send to New American Library, Rapture Romance Research Department, 1633 Broadway, New York, NY 10019.

RAPTURE ROMANCE

**Provocative and sensual,
passionate and tender—
the magic and mystery of love
in all its many guises**

Coming next month

WISH ON A STAR by Katherine Ransom. Fighting for independence from her rich, domineering father, Vanessa Hamilton fled to Maine—and into the arms of Rory McGee. Drawn to his strong masculinity, his sensuous kisses ignited her soul. But she had only just tasted her new-found freedom—was she willing to give herself to another forceful man?

FLIGHT OF FANCY by Maggie Osborne. A plane crash brought Samantha Adams and Luke Bannister together for a short, passionate time. But they were rivals in the air freight business, and even though Luke said he loved her and wanted to marry her, Samantha was unsure. Did Luke really want her—or was he only after Adams Air Freight?

ENCHANTED ENCORE by Rosalynn Carroll. Vicki Owens couldn't resist Patrick Wallingford's fiery embrace years ago, and now he was back reawakening a tantalizing ecstasy. Could she believe love was forever the second time around, or was he only using her to make another woman jealous?

A PUBLIC AFFAIR by Eleanor Frost. Barbara Danbury told herself not to trust rising political star Morgan Newman. But she was lost when he pledged his love to her in a night of passion. Then scandal shattered Morgan's ideal image and suddenly Barbara doubted everything—except her burning hunger for him. . . .

YOUR CHOICE OF TWO RAPTURE ROMANCE BOOK CLUB PACKAGES.

(A) Four Rapture Romances plus two Signet Regency Romances

or

(B) Four Rapture Romances, one Signet Regency Romance and one Scarlet Ribbons Romance

Whichever package you choose save $.60 off the combined cover prices plus get a free Rapture Romance, for a total savings of $2.55.

To start you off, we'll send you four books absolutely FREE The total value of all four books is $7.80, but they're yours *free* even if you never buy another book.

So order Rapture Romances today. And prepare to meet a different breed of man.

YOUR FIRST 4 BOOKS ARE FREE!

Just Mail The Coupon Below

Rapture Romance, P.O. Box 996, Greens Farms, CT 06436

Please send me the 4 Rapture Romances described in this ad FREE and without obligation. Unless you hear from me after I receive them, send me 6 NEW Romances to preview each month. I understand that you will bill me for only 5 of them with no shipping, handling or other charges. I always get one book FREE every month. There is no minimum number of books I must buy, and I can cancel at any time. The first 4 FREE books are mine to keep even if I never buy another book.

Each month please send me package ( )A   ( )B

Name	(please print)

Address	City

State	Zip	Signature (if under 18, parent or guardian must sign)

This offer, limited to one per household and not valid to present subscribers, expires June 30, 1984. Prices subject to change. Specific titles subject to availability. Allow a minimum of 4 weeks for delivery.

RAPTURE ROMANCE

**Provocative and sensual,
passionate and tender—
the magic and mystery of love
in all its many guises**

New Titles Available Now

(0451)

#61 ☐ **STERLING DECEPTIONS by JoAnn Robb.** Entranced by his seductive charm and beguiling blue eyes, Jan Baxter shared a memorable night of glorious passion with Dave Barrie. And though Jan wasn't convinced, Dave called it love—and swore he'd prove it. . . (128133—$1.95)*

#62 ☐ **BLUE RIBBON DAWN by Melinda McKenzie.** Billie Weston was swept into aristocrat Nicholas du Vremey's caressing arms and a joyous affair that tantalized her with the promise of love. But Nick's stuffy upper-class circle was far removed from Billy's own. Was the flaming passion they shared enough to overcome the gulf between their worlds? (128141—$1.95)*

#63 ☐ **RELUCTANT SURRENDER by Kathryn Kent.** Manager Marcy Jamison was headed straight for the top until Drew Bradford—with his seductive smile and Nordic blue eyes—swept all her management guidelines aside. And though he broke all her rules, he filled her with a very unmanageable desire. She wanted Drew—but was there room in her life for someone who persisted in doing things his own way. . . ?
(128672—$1.95)*

#64 ☐ **WRANGLER'S LADY by Deborah Benét.** Breanna Michaels wasn't prepared for the challenge of Skye Latimer—who'd never met a bronco he couldn't break, or a woman he couldn't master—for she found herself torn between outraged pride . . . and aroused passion. . . . (128680—$1.95)*

*Price is $2.25 in Canada

RAPTURE ROMANCE

Provocative and sensual, passionate and tender— the magic and mystery of love in all its many guises

---

**Buy them at your local
bookstore or use coupon
on next page for ordering.**

RAPTURE ROMANCE

Provocative and sensual, passionate and tender— the magic and mystery of love in all its many guises

RAPTURE ROMANCE

Provocative and sensual, passionate and tender—the magic and mystery of love in all its many guises

Buy them at your local
bookstore or use coupon
on last page for ordering.